------------HOT TREE PUBLISHING------------

For information, contact the publisher, Hot Tree Publishing.
www.hottreepublishing.com

EDITING: HOT TREE EDITING
COVER DESIGNER: SOXSATIONAL COVER ART
INTERIOR DESIGN: RMGraphX

ISBN: 978-1-925655-56-8

10 9 8 7 6 5 4 3 2 1

MORE FROM
AMY

THE SOUTHERN DEVOTION SERIES
For the Love of Gracie (#1)
Curves in the Road (#2)
Complicated Relationships (#3)

STANDALONES
Across the Way
A Little Spark

TRADE ME COLLECTION
Still You

*To my mom, the woman whose strength
and forgiving nature inspires me.*

CHAPTER ONE

"Chug! Chug! Chug! Chug!" my friends and colleagues all chant as I down my… well, I've lost count of the number of shots I've taken tonight. Normally I don't drink like a college frat boy, but it's a special occasion. My older brother, Harrison, is getting married. As the best man, I promised to show him the best time possible. We agreed there'd be no strippers, but getting shitfaced is a vital part of the evening plans.

"Samuel!" A feisty blonde throws her arms around my neck and plants a sloppy kiss on my lips. "I missed you, Sammy." Ugh. I despise being called Sammy. It makes me sound like a five-year-old. When guys do it, they get a punch in the face. When a woman does it, especially in a high-pitched coo, she causes me to lose all interest. Not even my brother gets away with it, mostly because if he calls me Sammy he knows I'll reciprocate by calling him Harry, which sounds like a dirty old man.

"Paulette, I've told you before…," I start to say as I remove her arms from my neck and peel her off my body. Each time I pull on her arms, she grips tighter.

"Don't call ya Sammy. Yeah, yeah, I know." Rolling her eyes, she smacks her gum while chewing like a cow. *Gross.* We went out on three dates a few months back, and after a horrible night in the sack, worst sex ever, I told her I didn't think we had anything in common. Truth be told, I didn't want to have it go that far, which probably explained the horrible sex, but she pursued me relentlessly. At the time, I was lonely, and she followed me around like a lost puppy, even tracking me down on my jogging routes as though it were by accident. She was kind of cute, and the guys pressured me into having a fling to get over my ex. I'm not proud of using her, but I tried to let her down as easy as possible.

"I'm celebrating with my brother tonight. It was nice to see you, but I need to get back to my friends." Dropping her hold on me, she walks away, fumbling on her six-inch heels like a newborn baby calf. Why women feel the need to kill their feet to impress men, I'll never understand. A woman in a pair of sneakers is equally as hot; at least they can walk in them easier.

Harrison tosses his arm across my shoulder. "Who was

that hottie?" His words slur a little.

"That was Paulette."

Harrison cringes at the sound of her name because he's heard all the horror stories. He makes a sound sort of like "blahoohaugh" as he shakes off the creep factor. Only two years apart in age, we grew up together as best friends, so there's nothing Harrison doesn't know about me. Paulette is something he'd like to forget; she has a fetish for toes, but not even a seminormal one. She admitted to me once about sniffing and licking her own feet as a form of masturbation. I can't think about it without feeling a thickness in my throat.

I grip his arm and chuckle. "I think it's time to get you home. Your fiancée will kill me if we don't bring you home in one piece, and you are so many sheets to the wind I lost count." The effects of the alcohol are blurring my eyesight now. I haven't been this drunk since college. "Could be my drunken self not being able to do math too. I called a cab, now let's go."

Lecturing my brother on being too drunk is laughable a few moments later when I don't notice the step outside the bar. I stumble forward, falling to the ground and catching myself on my right wrist, which makes an audible crack as I land. "Shit!"

Harrison stands there laughing his ass off at me as I try to stand up with no luck. Someone is spinning the world like a merry-go-round and I can't get off. An arm links through mine and, when I stand, my gaze locks with the pale green eyes of a tall, beautiful, blonde female with lips I want to taste. "Hi." Unable to stop them, I feel my eyebrows moving up and down in what is probably supposed to be sexy in my drunken mind, but from the crease in her forehead and scrunched-up nose, it reeks of creepy.

Instead of running for cover, she laughs. "Hey there. That looks rough. You'll probably want to get it checked out." I glance down to see my hand is swollen. It probably hurts, though the alcohol is masking the pain for me.

"Fuck." Letting go of my arm, she walks away with her friend, and I try to call after her. "Betty!" *Who the fuck is Betty?* "I meant pretty… lady…." Yep, my flirt is spot-on for a nice night spent in jail for pervy stalking. A wave and a giggle, followed by a furtive glance in my direction, and then she walks away.

"Did you see her, Harrison?" I slap my good hand down on my brother's shoulder.

"The chick you called Betty? Yeah, I did." Clearly, he's unaffected by her.

"I think I'm in love."

"I think that's the Jack talking," he deadpans.

Pushing my finger into my chest, I say, "That's the Sam talking." Wrinkling my nose, I look up to the side. "Who's Jack?"

Helping me off the sidewalk, Harrison says, "He's going to be your worst nightmare tomorrow."

I shiver. "Oh." And I quickly forget about Jack because my mind is wondering about Betty, or whoever she is. Maybe I'll see her again when I'm sober. Hopefully she has a horrible short-term memory. For now, I need to get my hand checked out.

After spending two hours in the emergency room tonight—well, morning—I end up passed out at my brother's apartment. Just a sprain with a stress fracture of my thumb, nothing too serious. They gave me a removable wrist splint and advised I take 800mg of ibuprofen every four hours as needed.

The wedding isn't until later this evening, so I have plenty of time to sleep. Or so I think when I don't bother setting an alarm.

The worst way to greet the day is being shaken awake.

"Get up, Sam. Now!" he screams in my ear. Rubbing my eyes, I squint to see the clock and notice it's after three.

"Damn, why are you screaming, Harrison?" As I focus on him, standing in front of me wearing a black tux with red tie and cummerbund, I realize my faux pas. "Oh fuck. The wedding!"

"Yeah, asshole. I have to be there in forty-five minutes, and you're the best man! It takes at least thirty minutes to get across town without traffic. You better start praying to some higher power asking that we make it there in time or you're going to have one angry sister-in-law."

As much as I love his fiancée, I know never to make her angry. She's gone full Hulk on me before.

Jumping out of bed, I sniff my armpits, groan, and say, "Dude, alcohol is seeping from my pores. Go on to the church. I'll grab a shower and be there in time. I promise." A wedding can still start if the best man is late. The groom is an essential factor.

"Screw that! Under the bathroom sink are some moist towelettes and cologne. Grab both and get in the car now. We'll cover the stink long enough to get through the ceremony. Your tux is downstairs, now let's go." My brother is frazzled, to put it mildly. Wedding days seem to be quite stressful. Not sure why I ever thought I'd want to have one myself.

In this very moment, I wear humiliation stronger than the stench of alcohol. I'm a bit of a clean freak, so having my hand down my shorts, washing my nuts as I ride down the street with my brother is close to my worst nightmare.

"Dude, do you really think anyone will be smelling your nuts? Focus on the pits and use cologne to mask the rest." Racing down the road, his eyes keep sliding to the rearview mirror, making sure I work my hardest to get ready.

"How did you ever get a woman with such hygiene?" Moist towelettes are my brother's answer to getting more sleep. He stays out late, snoozes the alarm an extra thirty minutes, and uses the sheets to cleanse his nether regions— his words, not mine.

His idea of cologne is also not the same as mine. The size of the bottle and the knowledge that my brother is a cheapskate assure me it will be the cheapest cologne ever. I take a sniff of the tip, then cough and dry heave.

"I can't wear this shit. I'll use extra deodorant." I rub it everywhere, no exaggeration. If I sweat even a little bit today, I'm covered. Thankfully, the deodorant seems to belong to his fiancée, so I smell baby powder fresh. Still a better smell than the cheap-ass cologne, which quite literally smells like toilet water. "I still think you guys should have done a *Star Wars*-themed wedding. If I could've worn a robe and gone as Obi-Wan, we'd have no issue."

"You were there when I pitched the idea to her. She wasn't going for it."

The day Harrison brought home his girlfriend, Carrie, I made the connection to the actors who played Han Solo and Princess Leia, Harrison Ford and Carrie Fisher. Since childhood, I've been obsessed with the entire *Star Wars* franchise. Harrison and I used to pretend we were in space; he was always Han and I was Luke. After we became friends, I started calling her Leia and she never got mad about it. So when Harrison proposed, I told him they had to do the theme wedding. He was ecstatic, ready to jump on the wedding planner bandwagon with lightsaber bouquets and guests in cosplay. One side as stormtroopers and the others would be the Jedi order. The moment he brought the idea up though, with the awesome suggestion of a gold bikini-clad bride, she shot him down right away.

She's been dreaming of the white dress and the red bridesmaid gowns for as long as she can remember. And Hell would freeze over before she wore a bikini in front of her friends and dressed as a slave at her wedding as she vowed to obey him—her exact words. Because of that speech, he suggested they write their own vows. Nowhere would he put the word "obey."

"Still think you should've tried harder."

"One day you can suggest it to your wife."

Low blow from the big bro. Two years ago, I proposed to the woman I loved, just to be turned down. She said she loved me, but the thought of being with me forever didn't appeal to her. It didn't take me long to get over her afterward. She's an insipid woman.

Carrie, however, is a sweet woman who I am excited to call my sister-in-law. Though for the last few months, she's gone full-on bridezilla, stomping on the wedding party with her giant lizard feet. I hope once the wedding stress passes she'll go back to the wonderful woman I consider a close friend.

"When I am lucky enough to find a woman as caring, thoughtful, and amazing as Carrie, I'll bring it up."

His smile fades as I basically lay the smackdown on him with my adult answer.

Score one point for the little bro.

CHAPTER
TWO

It's not every day your best friend from college calls you up at the extreme last minute to ask you to take her sister's place in her wedding. Less than three hours before the event. No rehearsal. Never been a bridesmaid or a bride.

The phone call doesn't leave me feeling warm and fuzzy. Carrie's sister missed her flight, and I live a short way from the church and happen to be her size. That's what it boils down to. Her sister and I share the same voluptuous curves, the way Carrie put it. What she means is we are both built like linebackers with broad shoulders and hips to match. I do have a great ass though. And it's not only an opinion, either; it's the most frequent compliment I receive.

"Jilli!" Carrie shouts ecstatically as she throws her arms around me. *Where was this jubilation for me when she was proposed to?* She's acting as though we've been besties and nothing has changed.

After allowing her to bounce up and down squealing in my ear, I finally push her away from me to reclaim my personal space.

Glancing around the room, I count four other girls in red dresses. "Looks like you've got quite a wedding party already. Why do you need me?" Granted, I say it with more attitude than intended, but in my defense, I didn't have the luxury of preparing for the cheerleader reunion.

Her eyes widen in shock. I fear I broke her when she stares at me as if I just asked her to burn her pompoms. "Harrison has four groomsmen and a best man. I have to have the same number of bridesmaids or it would be uneven."

Putting on a fake smile, I will my eyes not to roll into the back of my head where they might see my brain. "It'll be nice to finally meet your fiancé." *Since we haven't spoken since before you met him.* Something tells me she went through her phone book desperately seeking a size, not a name.

"He's wonderful, you'll love him! Oh, and I can introduce you to his brother. He's single." Wink wink, nudge nudge. Internally, I groan and my eyes start to roll backward. I force them to stare straight ahead with a smile on my face like a deranged-looking clown. Being fake happy for someone is hard for me.

"Where's my dress?"

She points at a chair holding a bloodred, backless with a giant bow right above my ass dress with a matching bow for the back of my hair. In my line of work, I already perform good deeds. Why should I put myself through more torture? I could abandon her and run for my own sanity.

"Help me, Jilli. You're my only hope," Carrie begs as she watches me cringe at the dress. Dammit. No poker face. I'll have to work on one.

I snort. "Nice *Star Wars* reference." Carrie ignores my compliment and flitters over to the rest of the ladies in red. "I'll get dressed now, I suppose," I mumble.

Back in college, we were roommates, which was how we eventually became friends. If we'd not been thrown together by the random computer gods, I'm not sure we'd have crossed paths. Carrie is sunshine and daisies, the high school cheerleader, the class president. Me? I was the quiet goth girl in high school. The loner who enjoyed movie nights at home over attending the football game or going on dates. She was my first friend in college. She convinced me to get out more, gave me a makeover, and basically changed who I was.

After college, I got a job I loved, which she would never understand. We lost touch after graduation. In three years, we've barely been Facebook friends. A Facebook post was actually how I found out about the pending nuptials. She posted a picture of her hand with the ring displayed and the congrats comments blew up her page, continuously showing in my feed.

I'm happy for Carrie finding her soul mate, but at the ripe old age of twenty-nine, I've begun to worry I'll never find mine. Everyone says I have plenty of time, but with each passing birthday, I lose a little more hope.

I was close to engaged once. When my job interfered with his sex life, he split. Apparently, he couldn't go a full week without sex. The man I thought was my prince was nothing more than a frog.

My job has become my life. After spending six years in college, I obtained my degree in accounting, only to never need it for my dream career. Whereas Carrie followed her degree immediately, leading her into a management position. People like Carrie don't get people like me. We might as well live on different planets. Carrie's not a bad person, she can be a great friend when you need one, but she's always been interested in making the most money she can. She used to rave about being a strong, powerful woman bringing home the bacon for her family one day. In no way is it a bad thing, but it's not me. I'd be happy working minimum wage as long as what I'm doing makes me happy.

Shrill voices of excited women are giving me a headache. Snatching up the dress, I open the closest door and step inside. Little did I know it was a closet. *Fuck.*

Carrie peeks inside after I shimmy into my crimson calamity. "Why are you in the closet?"

Going the joke route, I shrug. "You haven't seen me in a few years and my luck with guys hasn't been so great. I wasn't sure people would be okay with me liking girls now." No laughter, only a confused look as though she can't tell if

I'm serious or joking. "I'm kidding." Sort of. I'd thought of joining the other team after all my issues with men, but it's not in the cards for me. "I thought this was the bathroom. Can you zip me up?"

Once my dress is zipped, I notice it only goes to midcalf, whereas the rest of the girls' covered their ankles. Her sister and I may be the same width, but not the same height. Six-foot chicks aren't normal. *Nothing* about me is normal.

Standing in a row ready to walk down the aisle, I look like a teacher following her class. None of the girls are taller than five foot five. I have six inches to a foot on every one of them.

One thing to be grateful for is the man escorting me in, who has two inches on me. Finally, someone taller in the wedding party. He glances down at my shoes, ballet slippers, and then ahead at the girls in front of me in heels. "Wow. You're tall." *Oh good, an Einstein.*

This time the eye roll happens. I mumble, "No shit, Sherlock. Got any other mysteries you need to solve?"

"Damn, do you kiss your mother with that mouth?"

"My mom's dead." I feign a brokenhearted look, and it achieves the foot-in-mouth look of guilt I want. My mother lives up north and dates a guy half her age—she's perfectly fine. Watching pretty boy squirm for words is fun.

Linked arm in arm, we walk down the aisle to some random love song I don't recognize. In other words, it's not a selection from my heavy metal/goth playlist. Marilyn Manson, Rob Zombie, and Korn are on the playlist for my future wedding. Nothing about me fits society's definition of a "typical girl."

The ceremony is mushy sweet with gooey vows and sniffs from the audience as they become all weepy. Biting my lips hard, I hold back my laughter. When I glance up, I notice the pretty boy usher I came in with holding his smile back too. Suddenly it dawns on me that he isn't standing in the same place in line as I am. He's the best man, the one Carrie wants to hook me up with. I've forgotten his name already, or perhaps she never told me. He should've walked in with the maid of honor, but I guess they put him with me due to the height. Either way, I haven't made a good first impression with him.

During the reception, I try to sneak out, but Carrie makes an announcement that she wants all the groomsmen and bridesmaids to dance together. "Sam," pretty boy says as he reaches for me.

"Jillian. My friends call me Jilli."

"Nice to meet you, Jillian." He grins. *How cute. His asshole self is fluent in sarcasm, it seems.* I stick my tongue out at him before reluctantly taking his hand and following him to the dance floor.

As he pulls me close, I inhale the scent of baby powder. "You smell like a chick."

"Thanks," he replies with a grin, then whispers, "Late night, had to use Carrie's deodorant in lieu of a shower. Trust me, the smell could be worse."

"It's a good smell, just not what I expected."

"Well, maybe you can catch me on a day after I've showered and inhale my normal scent." He scrunches his face up. "That sounded weird. You know what I mean."

I laugh and nod.

"What did you do to your hand?" Before he can answer, I say, "Wait, let me guess. Drunken spill during the bachelor party?"

"It was you! I knew you seemed familiar. I was so wasted last night I barely recognize myself today."

His face rang familiar to me earlier, but I couldn't place it. I hadn't made the connection that he was the drunk guy I'd lifted off the sidewalk until I noticed his splint when he asked me to dance. It's on the opposite arm he used to walk me down the aisle.

"You're welcome. Glad you took my advice too."

He reaches inside his coat pocket and pulls out a pen. "Sign my splint?"

"Usually people sign casts, not splints."

My comment doesn't faze him; he simply shrugs and hands over the pen.

"Why are you carrying a pen in your tux?"

"Occupational hazard," he responds, with no clarification. I write on the splint: *Glad you didn't trip walking me down the aisle. – Jillian*

"Can I cut in, Sammy?" bridesmaid number three requests. I didn't bother to learn her name.

"Please don't call me Sammy."

The cringe on Sam's face begs me to keep dancing with him. So naturally I step back. "You two enjoy!" I toss him a wink, and he flips me off behind her back.

CHAPTER
THREE

SAM

Nothing irritates me more than being called Sammy. Amelia knows this because she's been friends with Harrison since my childhood. My signal to Jillian hadn't been missed. I knew she caught on to my look begging her to keep dancing with me. Instead of saving me, she walks away, winks at me, and gives me a grin. Her playful nature, matching my sarcastic wit, intrigues me. Reluctantly, I dance with Amelia—without taking my eyes off Jillian across the room.

Though we'd barely talked, there are many things I already like about her. The way she struggles to sit in her dress tells me she's more of a T-shirt and jeans kind of girl. When she went up to the bar, she didn't grab a glass of champagne or wine, snagging a bottle of beer instead. And in less than a minute, she waves the bartender down for beer number two.

For two songs, Amelia yaps away in my ear while I stare at Jillian across the room. Seated at the bar, she props one leg up on the stool next to her, causing the slit of the dress to fall open, revealing a long, muscular leg. A guy tries to chat her up and cop a feel on her thigh at the same time. She places her leg on the floor and towers over him as she stands. His hands come up in surrender while he backs up slowly. When I chuckle at the sight, Amelia stops talking finally. "It's funny, right?" she asks. My laugh was apparently well timed to whatever she's saying, so I nod, and she continues talking again—unfortunately.

Jillian's gaze moves my way, and I make a silent plea for her to rescue me. She only waves and smiles before flagging the bartender for her third beer. She can toss them back like no woman I've ever known.

"Amelia, it's been lovely, but I need to dance with my new sister-in-law. Excuse me, please." Letting go isn't her strong suit; I practically have to tear her from my arms and move away before she clings back to me.

"Leia, may I have this dance, please?"

Carrie laughs as she takes my arm and follows me out to the dance floor. "Only you get to call me Leia, bro." Her hand resting on my shoulder, her elbow falls against my arm. "Amelia wasn't the bridesmaid I expected you to be attracted to."

"She was the one attracted to me, like a magnet. I could

barely pry her loose." Carrie chuckles softly in my ear. "I was curious about the late addition though, the one who wasn't in rehearsal."

"Jilli?" I nod. "Now *she's* your type. We were best friends in college. Honestly, I haven't spoken to her in three years, but when my sister couldn't make it, she was the first one I thought of. I'm ashamed I didn't think of her sooner. I get the vibe that she feels like an afterthought." Carrie turns her head with a sad smile directed at Jillian. "She was my first friend in college. I left high school as the top dog and entered college as nothing. We were polar opposites, but she let me in."

"Tough egg to crack?"

"The toughest. She's thick-skinned but the most loyal friend you could ask for. She hates wearing dresses, but she showed up today with only a few hours' notice, even though I never told her personally that I was even engaged. She had every right to tell me to go to hell." The pace of the song picks up, so I give Carrie a twirl and pull her back against me. Her laugh tinkles across the room, apparently reaching Jillian's ears as she turns to notice us. "You're showing off now. I know you too well." Another twirl, her arms out at her sides that time, and Harrison grabs her back for the rest of the dance.

My sister-in-law gave me some great insight and piqued my interest even more over this long-legged beauty. The bartender flips the top of a beer and hands it to Jillian as I walk up. "That's number four, isn't it?"

"You keeping tabs on me?" Her eyes sparkle with

interest behind the bottle hiding her plump lips. "Bartender, he'd like to catch up." *Hair of the dog.* My hangover is still rather fresh, but what the hell. It's supposed to be the best cure.

"Dance with me again?"

"Why?" No doubt she's a tough one.

"Because I'd like to dance with you. No ulterior motives."

After finishing off the fourth beer, she sighs and reaches out. The song changes to a slow romantic tune.

She eyes me curiously, her finger pointing upward as though the music floats above us. "Did you plan this?"

"I've been on the dance floor for the past four songs. How would I have planned it?" Pulling her against my body, I breathe in the sweet smell of vanilla on her skin. Long arms drape over my shoulders, and her hands press against my back. Each breath she takes draws my attention to her breasts. The temperature in the room heightens as our bodies sway together. Allowing my hands to travel down her naked back, I stop just above her ass. Her skin is so soft, so smooth. "You smell amazing," I whisper against her ear.

"Thanks." One word said in a way that might have given me pause if I couldn't feel her body shiver. Her involuntary body language can't be faked as easily as her tone. She wants me as much as I want her, that's plain to see, but she's fighting the attraction. "I need to go," she says, pulling away from me just before the song ends. She hustles through the crowd and out the door.

"You can run, but I'm going to chase you," I say to

myself as I watch her go. There's something special about her, and I'm not giving up so easily on finding out what it is.

CHAPTER
FOUR

JILLIAN

Dancing with Sam the second time stirs something in me that I'm not ready to face. When he whispers in my ear, it sends shivers across my skin, racing from head to toe. The last time I found myself attracted to a man this way, he broke my heart.

Four beers aren't nearly enough to intoxicate me, but being a responsible adult, I call a taxi to take me home to my cozy three-bedroom cottage east of town. Only a little more than a thousand square feet, at times the quiet makes it feel the size of a mansion. I convince myself that the loneliness heightens my reaction to Sam's attention. Denial is a superpower of mine.

Since I'd left the wedding early, I missed out on cake, and I was so busy trying to quell my nervousness with beer that I'd forgotten to eat. My stomach growls loudly. Searching through the fridge, I discover I have hardly any food on hand. Bread, cheese, and butter are available though, so I start up some grilled cheese. While the skillet's heating, I unzip the dress and fling it over the chair in the kitchen. Standing in a bra and panties, I butter bread and slap two pieces of cheese between them before tossing the sandwich on the skillet. I take off running to the other side of the house and grab a tank and shorts, making it back to the kitchen in time to flip the sandwich, and slip on my clothes while the second side browns.

My house mocks me with the table for four and extra bedroom sitting empty. As I sit eating my amazing grilled cheese in my empty kitchen, I wish falling in love would be easy. I wanted to let Sam in tonight, ached to know what his lips taste like, but fear always wins out.

My phone rings, displaying Carrie's number. I pick it up slowly, wondering why she would be calling me right now. "Hello?"

"Hey, Jillian." Her voice is a little shaky, and there is a lot of noise in the background.

"Shouldn't you be on your honeymoon?"

"We're at the airport. I wanted to personally thank you for showing up tonight. It meant a lot to me." There is enough emotion in her voice to let me know she's being genuine. *Maybe she is still the girl I knew in college.*

"You made a beautiful bride. Thanks for thinking of me

and letting me be a part of your special day."

"Let's get together for lunch one day after the honeymoon, okay? I love you, Jilli."

"Sounds good. I love you too, Carrie." We say our goodbyes and hang up.

Even if I had been an afterthought, I do love Carrie. And most of my friends are men now, so I could definitely use a girlfriend in my life again. What could it hurt to have lunch? If she keeps her promise, of course.

Early the next morning, I awake when someone knocks on my front door. Rolling over to peek at the clock, I groan at seeing it's after ten—not as early as I thought. I peer through the peephole and then glance down at my outfit. It's my neighbor Stephan outside the door. Considering he's seen me in a bikini when I sunbathe at his house, I'm not worried about him seeing me so scantily dressed. Opening the door, I ask, "What's up, Stephan?"

"Damn, girl, I constantly wonder why you're single." His eyes drift to my breasts, where most guys consider eye contact to begin.

"Yet you've never tried to date me." When I first moved in, he flirted a little, but it never went anywhere. After he had his pool installed, he invited me over to swim and was a perfect gentleman. In a way, I was a little offended because he had a rotating door of girls coming into his house. I thought it meant he wasn't attracted to me, and I'll admit, that stung a bit.

"Because you're a sweet girl and deserve better than a player like me. Can I come in?" He doesn't wait for an answer, stepping around me and heading straight for the kitchen. "I have a girl coming over tonight, and I need to borrow something. Do you have food?"

I laugh. We have a bit of an agreement that I can use his pool whenever I want. I even have a spare key to his house so, when he's out of town for work, I can help myself and feed his cat, Scooter. In return, I help him impress his conquests with cooking or baking. "Why don't you order takeout, like a normal person who doesn't cook?"

Grinning mischievously, he admits, "Because I told her I was a gourmet cook." Before I could ask where the lie came from, he adds, "I was in the grocery store and I spotted this gorgeous redhead in the spice aisle. I needed to bump into her, so I pretended to be checking for certain spices. I now have a kitchen full of exotic spices with nothing to spice. Please help me out?"

"You're unbelievable, and not in a good way. How long until she arrives?"

"Three hours."

"Let's make a run to the store. I'll help you make dinner and be gone before she arrives. Deal?" Stephan grins widely and grabs me up in a tight hug. "You owe me, just so you know."

A fresh fruit and vegetables stand five minutes from my house is the first stop. I could grab all this stuff at the store too, but I like supporting local farmers. After making our rounds, we load the car with bags of tomatoes, fresh greens, and carrots, then head to the grocery store. "I hope she's worth all the dough you're going to spend on this meal."

Turning to the butcher, I say, "I need two large chicken breasts, please."

"Make that three, please." Stephan turns to me. "You can make a plate to go. One thing is for sure, I have every spice you could imagine."

When we get back to his house a few minutes later, I find out he isn't exaggerating. One shelf of a cabinet holds around ten to fifteen various spices. A couple of them are ridiculously expensive, ones that only rich, exotic recipes call for. Although, Stephan can swing it. You can't tell by the small house he lives in, but he's loaded. He lives below his means on purpose. No one can call him a tightwad though; his philosophy is he'd rather spend money to explore the world instead of on material things such as a house he could get lost in.

A few years ago, he developed an app for schools, which has now gone international. Most of his travels are for teaching schools how to utilize the app to suit their needs. After he made his first million, he took me out to celebrate. I thought for sure he'd move into a bigger neighborhood after, but I'm glad he never did.

When he discovered that I'd graduated with an accounting degree I don't use, he had me work his finances until it became a full-time gig. I'm not willing to give up my day job to be his personal accountant, but he said I would have a job if I ever decide it's what I want to do.

"What the hell are you ever going to do with all of these?"

"Have you over for dinner more?" Stephan winks at me.

If he wasn't terrified of commitment, I might consider dating him. Then again, I sort of like having someone close to me without any worries of intimacy.

"Get to work washing vegetables." If I'm going to make his dinner, he's going to put some energy into it as well. "If you help me wash and cut, you can honestly tell the girl you made dinner. I'll walk you through everything." I pause for a moment, then murmur, "You should consider settling down, Stephan."

He pops a few clean cherry tomatoes into his mouth while chopping the carrots and cucumbers for the salad.

"Maybe one day when I'm older."

"You're thirty-five. What age is old enough for love?" Hell, I'm six years younger than him and freaking out already about being alone. No, I don't *need* a man to be happy, but I want a relationship. I enjoy how I feel when I'm part of one.

I want that feeling again.

With fifteen minutes to spare, dinner is ready. We set the table with plates, silverware, napkins, and candles. Stephan fills a Tupperware bowl for me with a piece of chicken, green beans, and a salad. I squirt a little dressing on the side and turn to leave.

The doorbell rings.

"Shit. She's early." Stephan pleads with me, and I know what he's asking.

I nod silently, and he mouths, "Thank you!"

I grab a plastic bag to set my food in. Stephan never uses the side fence because it stays jammed closed. Now I will essentially get to climb my way out of the yard with my plate of food. Luckily, there are trash cans on the opposite side of the fence, so at least it'll be a little easier. I grab a bucket, turn it over, and step up on top of it. Tossing my bag of food onto the garbage cans, I hoist myself up on the fence and climb over the top, bracing myself on the trash cans and then dropping down to the ground. Stephan is in my debt big-time for my sacrifices tonight to help his weekly booty call go down without a hitch.

Once again, I find myself sitting alone in the house, eating at the dining table while quietly reading on my e-reader. Why does life seem so much lonelier when you meet someone who interests you? After dinner, I wash Stephan's Tupperware dish, which I will return the next day when he comes by to brag about his conquest. It has been a terribly long day, and I only have one more day to sleep in before going back to work.

Shortly after 1:00 a.m., my phone starts ringing. Everyone is being called in to work for an emergency. An apartment complex is on fire, and they need everyone on hand due to the number of people who could be affected by it. Caffeine couldn't wake me up nearly as fast as the adrenaline from saving lives.

Being woken in the middle of the night is often part of my job. For this reason, I always pick out clothes for the next day and lay them out on the chair next to the bed so they're easily accessible. I throw on my clothes, pull my hair up into a ponytail, and slip my shoes on. Within a few minutes, I'm in the car on my way to work. A ten-minute drive most days, but during emergencies, I get there in seven.

Stepping out of my car, I smell the smoke in the air and rush inside to change.

CHAPTER
FIVE

After the wedding, I take a few days off work to rest my wrist and take advantage of the sleeping pills I've neglected. The doctor gave me a prescription a few months back to help with my insomnia, but I hate the way they make me feel. I have weird dreams when I take them, and one night my neighbor had to babysit me after I walked outside with nothing on at all. She works the night shift and was just coming home from work. Probably not how she wanted to be greeted after a long day.

The doctor warned me that the sleeping pills affect people in different ways. For me they cause a dense fog of uncertainty of my surroundings, the time of day, where

I am—and whether or not I'm appropriately dressed for public, apparently.

Tonight I wake up to a loud beeping sound. Rolling over, I smack my hand against the alarm, trying to silence the annoying thing, but it won't stop. I place the pillow over my head to drown out the noise, but it's almost immediately yanked away, and I see a large creature with no face but a set of green eyes staring down at me. Its mouth is moving, though I can't make out the words.

"I'm packing heat! You won't take me alive!" I yell out.

It lurches forward to pull me from my bed, and I scream and try to kick my way free. Quickly losing the fight, my arms grow tired and the large creature lifts me from the bed, throws my arm around their shoulder, and carries me through a thick stream of smoke. Suddenly the heat around us is intense. *Was it like that before?*

My throat begins to close, and it's growing harder to breathe, but the creature won't release me to the ground. He's taking me to his leader as more faceless creatures surround me and one lifts me onto a bed.

"I was comfier in my own bed. Don't take me to the portal, please."

Deep voices converse around me, but I can't understand their language. Either I'm going mad, having a crazy dream, or… well, there doesn't seem to be any more options.

One of the long-armed creatures removes his faceless mask to reveal a bald head, his kind eyes finding mine.

"You're a big dude," I mumble as he chuckles. "You look human."

He reaches across my face to put a contraption over my mouth so I can't speak. I thrash my head from side to side, trying to stop him, but he's too strong for me. Then I drift into darkness. The alien creatures are going to have their way with me now. At least I'll be asleep and will miss the probing or whatever else happens.

Sometime later, I wake up, unsure of how much time has passed. The beeping noise starts once more. I reach out to slap my alarm clock and hit a solid surface.

"Whatcha looking for, honey?" a woman's southern voice rings out, full of charm.

Jerking forward, I yell, "Why are you in my bedroom?" I grab the sheet to cover myself. My eyes search the bare white walls around me until they land on the machines to my right and then my left. Glancing down, I notice my usual *lack* of sleep-time attire is now a pale blue gown with tiny dark blue dots.

Fuck. I'm in a hospital.

"What did I do?"

She slips a finger cuff on me, the machine in her hand beeps, and she writes the number down. "Your apartment complex caught on fire last night. You were brought here for observation because you suffered a little smoke inhalation, but nothing too severe. The doctor will be in shortly to give you a short examination, and then she'll most likely release you."

"A fire? I don't remember anything."

"You were apparently on some pretty good sleeping pills. You tried to sleep through the entire thing. Luckily, the firefighters reached your apartment in time. One of them saved you. You're a lucky guy. Your neighbor told them he hadn't seen you in days, so they almost passed you up."

I usually sleep in the nude, so whoever the guy is probably got quite a show from me. Still, I want to show my gratitude. Knowing I could have died last night is scary. And now I may not have a home anymore.

"Can I meet my savior? Is there a way to find out who it was?"

Convinced my neighbor tried to let me die, I want to thank the person who foiled his plans. We've never been close and he's completely paranoid, absolutely sure that I persuaded his wife to leave him since she and I are friends. She's a smart woman—all I did was help her find a place to live when she left him. No convincing needed there.

"I'll see what I can find out."

The details of my abduction last night grow clearer in my mind. The aliens must have been firemen, which means I said some crazy things to them. Although, they're most likely used to craziness in their line of work. If nothing else, I gave them a good story to tell.

Two hours go by before the doctor shows up to discharge me. They give me a set of scrubs to wear home since I came without any clothes. After signing off, the nurse escorts me out the door in a wheelchair—not that I need it, of course, but hospital policy and all that—and I stand up to thank her once we're outside. As I turn around, Jillian walks toward me.

"What are you doing here?" I scowl at her more than I

mean to. Snarky comments are not what I need right now.

Her smile fades, and she turns her attention to the nurse. "Hello, Marcia. It's nice to see you again. I'm sorry you're always getting the trouble patients."

"Go easy on him, Lieutenant Hartford. I think he's a bit embarrassed about how he acted while on meds." Nurse Marcia waves goodbye, leaving me with my shame.

"Lieutenant? You're in the Army?" Admittedly, the concept isn't crazy for the woman. For someone of her stature, it seems like a natural choice.

"No, I'm a firefighter. I was called here because I was informed you wanted to meet the person who saved you." Her eyes widen as she leans her head forward and to the side as though waiting to hear a gasp of surprise, which comes a moment later as her words register.

"*You* saved me?" The words literally squeak out of my throat, making me sound like a prepubescent boy. "Wait. What was I wearing?" I was hoping, by some miracle, the sleeping pills kept me from undressing for a change.

A blush creeps across her cheeks, which is a charming response for someone who, since the moment we met, maintains a scowl and speaks sarcasm fluently. "Let's just say that, if it wasn't your birthday, you were wearing the wrong suit for the occasion."

Cringe. Blush. Dive for cover from embarrassment. A beautiful, strong, sexy, funny woman saw me in the most vulnerable state I've ever been in. Not the naked part, of course—I look damn good naked—but the doped-up period.

"And after you carried me outside?"

"I didn't carry you, just assisted you. Me and my alien buddies, that is." A smirk graces her lips and more details of my dream come back.

"What did I do? What did I say?"

"How about I give you a ride home and fill you in on everything?" she offers.

The fact I'd been brought to the hospital by ambulance completely slipped my mind. The nurse must have assumed someone was coming to get me.

"Is my apartment building still standing?"

"Crap. Not entirely. It's not livable, at least, but for the most part, your section of the building only had smoke damage. Most of your things should be fine. You have to wait until they clear you to go back in though. If you need a place to stay, I have a couch." The way her voice changes when she makes the offer tells me she is trying desperately to be nice, but isn't necessarily sincere about letting me crash at her place.

"You don't even know me. Why would you offer a stranger your couch?" The first time she's actually inviting me in, and I'm questioning it? If I wouldn't look crazy in front of her, I'd kick my own ass right now.

"Carrie says you're a good man. Besides, I know how to protect myself."

"Harrison and Carrie won't be back for a few days. I can stay at their place. If you don't mind dropping me off, I can give you some money for gas."

As she seems to consider the request, I take a moment to ogle her. The pale blue tank top she's wearing clings to her breasts, though the button-down shirt over it hides her figure. The shirt is buttoned from the middle section down and goes halfway to her knees, so I won't be able to check out her ass. The smell of coconut coats the air around us; I wonder if it's her shampoo, or maybe a perfume or body lotion. What I wouldn't give to be close enough to figure it out for myself.

"Why don't you buy me breakfast instead, and we can talk more."

She seems to be trying to find excuses for us to spend time together. I like where this is leading.

Harrison's apartment is only twenty minutes from the hospital. Along the way, we stop at a bakery and buy a few pastries to have with coffee, choosing a small table toward the back

"Are you sure you want to know about yesterday?" She sips on her coffee, glancing up at me over the cup from her seat across the table from me. "The boys know you took sleeping pills and were unaware of your surroundings. It's nothing we haven't seen before."

The subtle smile she is actively trying to control says she's dying to rub the way I'd acted in my face. *Why not give the woman a moment of pleasure?* Her peridot-colored eyes bore into mine, making it hard to concentrate on anything anyway. What's a little humiliation between nonfriends?

"Just tell me."

"I leaned over you to wake you up, but you were pretty much dead to the world. Your chest was moving up and down, so I knew you were breathing. When you finally startled awake, you jerked up in the bed, sending the covers flying. You—" Jillian cleared her throat. "—saluted me."

Shit.

"Sorry."

"Don't be." She giggles, then blushes and clears her throat again. "You grabbed it and told me you were packing heat and wouldn't be taken alive."

I need her to stop now. It can only get worse from here.

"I half-assed grabbed a towel to cover your waist and helped you outside. My captain took over for me, and you attacked him."

"Oh shit. Was he hurt?"

She busts out laughing as she shakes her head, gasping for breath. Finally able to speak once again, she says, "Your arms were flailing around like a little girl having a slap fight." The last few words come out in gasps of laughter. "All he had to do was use one finger to hold you down."

At least one thing is sure to me in the moment: she's never going to see me naked again, because I'm the butt of a joke to her. "I probably held back so I wouldn't hurt him."

Coffee flies from her mouth, smacking me in the face and soaking my shirt as she chokes out more laughter. "You wouldn't have hurt a fly with those moves!"

As her laughter grows louder, with no end in sight, I cross my arms over my chest, holding back a pout of embarrassment as best I can. Once she calms down, I ask, "Are you finished laughing at my expense now?"

"I'm sorry. You're right, I shouldn't make fun of you." She barks out one more laugh. "But if you could've seen it.

If it had been someone other than you, it would be hysterical, don't you think?"

"Perhaps. In this case it *was* me, so we'll never know." The revelation that she's here because she saved my life and I owe her gratitude comes to me before I can throw any sarcastic wit her way. But I really want to.

"The nurse said you went against orders to leave my apartment alone. Did you know I was the one who lived there?"

She shakes her head. "To a degree, we rely on neighbors to help us determine how much of a risk we should take. Your neighbor said he hadn't seen you in several days, but the fire hadn't reached your unit yet, so I made a decision to check anyway. I'm glad I did."

Awkwardly fidgeting with her shirt, she looks away from me. Suddenly the room heats up. Our playful banter subsides. From the outside looking in, it may appear that we have a mutual distaste for the other, but my gentle teasing is an act of adoration.

Harrison and I own our own real estate business, and we've been rather successful in the past couple of years. With success comes long hours and little free time for love. When I was with Anya, my almost fiancée, I wanted to marry her, but I'm not sure if it was love or just a way of not being alone. Since she demolished our relationship, I work the club scene, and most of the girls I meet are vapid or, even worse, incredibly vain. Jillian is neither. Finding out she's a lieutenant firefighter might turn some guys off, thinking she can outdo their toughness, but to me, it's damn sexy.

She matches my wit, my strength, and my good looks. It's confidence, not ego.

Saving the damsel in distress, being the superhero, is what many men strive to do. I'm no different. But strong women, not only physically but emotionally, are sexier than anything. Too many women I've met wanted to play the victim out of fear of turning me off. The woman in front of me, she is fearless.

"What is your occupation?" she asks.

"What?" It isn't the question but the wording that throws me for a loop.

"When you had a pen in your tux, you said 'occupational hazard.'"

That she remembers something so trivial from a conversation we had a few days ago means she's been thinking about me. Her eyes drift down to my splint. *Or it means she sees her signature and it rings a bell.* I prefer to go with the first theory.

"I sell real estate. Harrison and I run our company together. Warner Brothers Real Estate." Her eyebrows rise, and she smiles. "Yes, I know. It's why we spell out 'brothers' instead of abbreviating so we don't get sued."

She leans forward with sudden interest. "Really? I find that fascinating. Can I tell you a secret?"

You can tell me everything. "Sure" is my only reply.

"One of my favorite hobbies is looking at homes. I window-shop for houses. One day I'll find my dream one." She pauses and places her hand over her mouth. "Too weird, isn't it?"

"No, it's just…." Considering the wordage in my head first, it takes me a moment before I say, "You're a pet peeve of our business." She arches one eyebrow in question, so I go for the first thought I have, which in retrospect isn't the best. "You waste the realtor's time by looking at houses you don't plan to buy."

Crossing her arms over her chest, she sits back and glares at me. "I don't buy everything I look at in the mall either. That doesn't mean I'm wasting the cashier's time."

And the argument never stops between us, it seems. "I'm kind of tired now and would like to go see what's left of my home." If I end this early tonight, maybe we can hang out another time without having a fight looming over us.

"You'll have to wait a few days for the area to be cleared. I can drive by there, but we can't go in."

"Just take me home for now." With our latest argument still fresh, I thought it best not to prolong this day.

We leave the coffee shop, and the drive to Harrison's is filled with uncomfortable silence. Jillian walks me to the door and opens her mouth to speak, but I cut her off. "Thanks for saving me, I guess." I don't know why I added the "I guess." All I want is for her to come inside and start over with me, but I can see the hurt in her eyes before she responds.

"The sincerity from you is endearing. If all my rescues were as grateful as you, I'd probably quit my job."

The fight I want to avoid is now inevitable. My mouth keeps spouting words before my brain can think them over. At least neither of us is acting mature right now, so it's not just me.

Shoving open the door, her strength forces it against the wall, leaving a small dent in the paint.

"Thanks. I'm sure my brother will appreciate having to repaint now."

"For one freaking notch? So that's what the insipid Carrie sees in him. He's as petty as she's become."

No matter how much I try to distract her, she keeps hitting my buttons. And through my anger, I'm still finding myself wildly attracted to her.

"I thought you two were best friends in college?" For the life of me, I can't figure out where we go wrong every time we meet. We're having a nice conversation, getting to know each other, and then *wham*, we're at each other's throats. And somehow I can't stop thinking about kissing her.

"I was a fill-in for her sister because we happen to wear the same dress size. She's become quite the narcissist since I knew her in college."

"She was a bridezilla for her wedding, yes, but that woman has been a godsend to my brother. She's been a best friend to me. She told me at the wedding that she felt bad for not keeping in touch with you. Sounds like you're the arrogant one to me." My words are angry, but looking at her, all I want is to press her against the wall and kiss her senseless. The firm line of her lips begs me to taste them. Her eyes might be angry, but they have lust in them as well. She feels the passion between us just as strongly as I do.

So why are we sitting here screaming across the room at each other?

Jillian steps toward the door, and I wrap my fingers around her wrist, pulling her into my arms. Swinging her around, I jerk her forward and our lips crash together. Instead of fighting it, she melts into me and her body relaxes. When I slip my tongue between her lips, she groans and her teeth tug on my lower lip.

A first kiss has never made me so hard. Then again, there's no one else I enjoy fighting with as much as her either. I guess they're right about sexual tension making for great passion. Thinking with my dick, I want to rip her clothes off right now, but instead I use my brain—though it's not that easy, the difficult fight ensuing between my brain and dick intense. My brain whispers for me to take this slow, and dammit if my dick isn't making slow a foreign word.

Jillian takes charge over the moment, which is sexy as hell. Her hands drop from around my chest and immediately go to work on the string of the scrub pants.

"Whoa, whoa. Slow down." The voice resembles mine, but my dick is confused when the words spill forth from my lips. I think I even heard a "what the hell" from somewhere. Apparently, my brain gained control after all. Good for him, I guess.

She slaps her hand over her mouth, her eyes widening as she steps back from me. "I'm… I need to go."

"Wait!" But my face meets with a slammed door. By the time I get it open once more, she's climbing in her car.

Instinctively, I run to my phone to text her and find out what's wrong.

Then I realize she never gave me her number.

CHAPTER SIX

"Good job, Jilli! Attack your former best friend's new brother-in-law as though you're a sex-starved maniac!" The maniac part is certainly correct as I fly down the interstate yelling at myself.

Thank goodness I never gave him my number. Though it's not as if he'd use it even if I did because I'm a nutbag. A total loon. My cornbread isn't cooked thoroughly in the middle. Not sure about the colloquialism—I read it in a meme recently—but it sounds like it'd fit here.

Being the only female firefighter in my crew, I have to be tough to keep up with them. No way will I sit here and cry over some man who barely matters. The few conversations we've had were full of sarcasm or annoyance. That kiss though… it was beyond any rush I've experienced in my life.

And my erratic driving leads me back to where I saw Sam just before the kiss—the hospital. Nothing is wrong with me, physically, but I need a good dose of Adam. Adam is an ER doctor I'd gotten to know in my years of fighting fires and bringing in trauma victims for him to treat. One day we started a conversation, and whenever I'm having a moment, he's always willing to listen.

Me: Is it about time for you to take a break? I need to talk.

Adam: In fact it is. I have an hour free. Where are you?

Me: Outside in the parking lot.

Adam: Stalker.

Just as his message comes through, he appears outside and lifts his hand in a wave before he sprints across the lot. Sliding in the car, he leans over and gives me a kiss on the cheek. "You're welcome to talk to me, but I need serious Mexican food. Let's go down the street."

We are immediately seated at a table for two in the corner where we have some privacy. The waitress winks at me, probably assuming we're on a date. She doesn't know Adam plays for the opposing team.

Stabbing his fork almost maliciously around the bowl, he sighs after his first bite. "I love that I can order a salad and pretend it's healthy even though they bring it out to me in a deep-fried bowl reminding me it's not with its beautiful buttery flavor. God bless Americanized Mexican food."

"Amen!" We clink our forks together in solidarity. "So how are things with Mr. Wonderful?"

Adam closes his eyes and sighs in contentment again. "Freaking amazing."

"I'm jealous. You are my inspiration for love. You two have such a dream story."

Coughing on a bit of salad, he spits, "Dream? Sure, if you call misunderstandings and losing touch for six months a dream."

"The dream part is that, after all that time, you found your way back to one another." Pressing my hand against my forehead, I feel it crease with the confused expression I wear.

"You okay?"

"Do I have a fever?"

Placing the back of his hand against my forehead, he shakes his head.

"Are you feeling ill?" he asks.

"I must be. I don't normally get so smushy over love. What's happening to me?"

"Well, you picked me up for lunch on the spur of the moment, so I'm waiting to hear the answer myself."

Two years ago, after staying too long inside of a building, looking for a lost child, I ended up in the ER after passing out from heat exhaustion and smoke inhalation. Adam was my treating physician. Over the course of the evening, he checked in on me a few times and I could tell he was upset about something, so I asked what was wrong. He must have been waiting on someone to ask because his whole long, sad story spilled forth from his lips before I'd even finished my question.

After his shift, he stopped back by to check in once more and get to know me better. Now each time one of us needs to talk through something, we text a lunch or break request and meet up. He's the closest thing I have to a best friend, though we don't hang out on a regular basis. He's the person who knows me better than anyone lately.

"A man. A frustrating, pigheaded, fuckwit of a man who I am so incredibly attracted to that it's pissing me off." Love isn't something I stress over or even think about most days. My job revolves around saving things most precious to people: their loved ones, their homes, their pictures. I don't have time for love when I need to focus on those priorities.

"Sounds like you're finding out what love feels like."

"Oh please, I barely know anything about the guy except that he pushes every button I have, both the good and bad." Equally good and bad, though I will say the good buttons outweigh the bad with how memorable they can be.

"I knew I was in love with Eden the first time we sat down and talked about something other than bushes." Some might find a gay man talking about bushes rather odd, but he is in fact referring to an actual bush, his husband being a landscape architect.

"Sam is his name. And if this is love I'm feeling, well, it's not what I expected. We kissed once, and it was… violent?" Based on the cringe on his face "violent" probably isn't the word to use. "Not violent in a bad way."

"Wow. What violence to you *isn't* bad? Let's start this way. If you were an author, how would you describe the kiss?" He rolls his hands through the air, gesturing for me to begin.

"He ripped my arms forward and shoved his lips against my face." In my head, I can see the memory perfectly.

"Ripped your arms forward?" Adam shivers. "Does sound violent. And by the way, never write a book. At least not a romance novel."

After seeing Adam's reaction, I think back to my description and understand the horror. I never claimed to be a wordsmith.

"Violent wasn't the correct word to use."

"No shit, Sherlock." That's the same phrase I'd used on Sam when we first met at the wedding. Perhaps I spend more time with Adam than I realize.

"Here's the Fabio version, then. His eyes burned with passion as his soft hands grasped mine, pulling me roughly into his arms. As he fingered my hair, his eager lips caressed my aching mouth." My mom used to read Harlequin romances when I was younger, and occasionally I picked one up to peruse it.

"Stop, please. Never use 'fingering' in that way. Weird. And 'aching mouth'? What the fuck is a Fabio?"

No matter how I describe it, I couldn't do it justice or make it even sound desirable.

"Hot kiss. Tongue. Better?"

"Perfect." Adam winks and takes a bite of his salad, smiling as he chews. "Tell me why you're stressing about the hot kiss. Why is this guy so horrible?"

"He's not, and he is."

"One thing I love about you, you're so descriptive and not at all confusing or unclear."

Honesty is one of his most lovable qualities. When I need advice, I want real help, not a sugarcoated anecdote or cliché. Adam never fails me.

"What little I know about him is he's now the brother-in-law of my former best friend from college. I can't put into words how I feel because I don't know. Advice isn't really my goal here. I need a friend to let me vent to. It was probably stupid."

"Taco salad and venting are never stupid. Look, a hot kiss could be nothing more than the description says. But if you're feeling a twinge of loss being away from him, or wondering what he's feeling right now or if he's thinking about you in this moment, it's probably safe to say you're falling for him."

Simple words. If only love could be so simple.

My phone buzzes on the table, and Adam cocks an eyebrow as I read the message.

Sam: It's Sam. Save me as a contact.

Me: Who gave you my number?

Sam: Bridezilla.

Me: Why do you want it?

Sam: Is this Jillian?

Me: Yes?

Sam: That's why.

Me: Um…ok?

Sam: Just save my damn number.

Me: Saved, Sammy.

I intentionally push his buttons by calling him a nickname I know he despises. I grin while awaiting a snarky response. Much to my surprise, it's quite civil instead.

Sam: I'm going to call you tomorrow, and I really hope you will pick up so we can talk.

Me: If I'm not busy, we'll see.

Adam had been reading the texts over my shoulder. "You are such a tease. I'm glad I don't date women."

Rolling my eyes, I scoff. "I've heard your love story, remember? You were a bit of a tease yourself."

"Touché. Shit, is that really the time? I have to get back to work."

We flag the waitress down, and I grab the bill before Adam can. He huffs his disapproval but doesn't try to fight me.

"My treat. I needed this today." Even if he says nothing, Adam oozes confidence, and it's contagious. And a hefty dose of confidence is the best medicine for me to pursue Sam.

"You have to call me later and give me the scoop after you talk to him."

After dropping him off at the entrance to the emergency room, I wave goodbye and drive toward my house.

Living alone occasionally has its perks. I keep my windows and blinds shut so once inside, all the clothes come off and the bra is flung across the room at the speed of light. If I never had to wear a bra again, or worry about putting out my eye when I go running, I wouldn't wear the contraption. I've been single so long that I can't remember the last time I wore a pretty one. Nowadays my drawers are filled with cotton sports bras.

Though if Sam asks me out, I will strap on a lacy black push-up in a second. I smirk knowing how Adam would have reacted had I said "strap on" around him. I love being immature with him; it makes me forget about some of the suckiness of being an adult some days.

I barely slept with the anticipation of Sam's call. I have so much energy this morning, I clean my house from floor to ceiling. Rearranging the furniture three times before putting it back in almost exactly the same positions, I realize I need a fuller life. Almost everything in my life revolves around my job. Even my social life involves drinking with the men in my department. Being the only female, they are protective of me and always make sure I make it home safely if I drink too much. Our station is family. I was born an only child, but I have twelve brothers now. Still, it can get lonely when the majority of your friends are coworkers. No escape from work, even for an hour or two.

I turn on the television, cue up Netflix, and find a movie, which takes all of thirty seconds. The phone rings. And then it stops. And it rings again and stops again. The caller ID clearly shows Sam's name. It reminds me of when I was a teenager and I would try to get up the courage to call someone.

Grabbing life by the balls, I dial his number to hear it picked up, a woman giggling, some kissing noises mixed with moaning, and the click of the End button once more. *Seems he found someone to scratch his itch. Guess he no longer needs me.* Kissing and moaning noises replay in my head. The heat of my blood pressure skyrocketing colors my cheeks. The sting of rejection is one thing; this feels more like burns and stabs. *Why did he push so hard to get through to me? Does he really need me to be another notch in his belt? Well, fuck him. He isn't worth it.*

In my contacts, I click on his name, then Edit, scroll to the bottom and click Delete Contact. "So long, asshole."

Propping my feet on the table, I resume my Netflix and chill position, using the literal meaning, not the urban dictionary one. For the rest of the night, I drift away into *Hawaii Five-0*, the remake. Tonight I'll let the guy playing Steve McGarrett fill my fantasies. At least he knows how to pursue one woman at a time.

Maybe those guys only exist in stories.

CHAPTER
SEVEN

SAM

The plan had been to work half a day and call Jillian as soon as I got home from work, but that plan backfired. A client called asking me to show them a house, so I drove across town to meet them hoping it wouldn't take too long.

My client, Heather, has been searching for a two-bedroom house for months without luck. There is always something missing, the price is wrong, there's no garage, or the carpet is ugly. She didn't seem to comprehend that she could easily change the carpet. Until today, I was sure fear drove her pickiness. Now she's found the unicorn, the perfect two-bedroom house she's always dreamed of with no faults.

"Why didn't you answer your phone?" she shouts at me as I step from my vehicle. "I've been here for half an hour." That's the moment I realize I left my phone in my haste to get out here and hurry this along.

"Sorry, I must have left it at my brother's house." I punch in my realtor code and open the door, letting her stroll in first. But instead of a stroll, she practically leaps over the threshold and runs through each room before taking a breath.

"It's perfect. Put in an offer now. Go five over asking price if need be."

"Slow down, Heather. You should always try to get the best deal. Let's offer them a few under the asking price, and they can counter if they want."

She peruses the brochure in her hand. Her eyes drift upward, and I see her lips moving as she works the calculations in her mind for the mortgage payment.

"I want to at least offer full price. I don't want them to turn me down. I've been searching for this house for too long already. I want it, and as soon as we close on it, I can propose to my girlfriend and present it to her."

After hearing those words, how could I deny her?

The seller is a friend of mine, so I borrow her phone to call him up and tell him our offer. Taking a seat at the stage table in the dining room, I open my briefcase and pull out the necessary paperwork. "So, the selling realtor is going to speak with his clients as soon as he receives the paperwork. He has had one other offer, but it was a low one, so you have a good shot. Let's fill these out quickly, and I'll stop by the office and get them faxed over to him so he can get back with us."

Thirty minutes later, all the paperwork has been filled out and signed for the offer. She also gives me instructions for counteroffers to make it go quicker, if necessary. "You'll have to be sure and invite me to the wedding." I escort her outside and lock the door.

"Thank you so much, Sammy."

Ugh, why do people insist on calling me Sammy?

"Sam. And you're welcome, Heather. I need to run. If you have any questions or concerns, let me know. Otherwise, I'll be in touch with you as soon as I hear back on the offer. They only have forty-eight hours to respond." Making the sale is always important to me, and normally I would spend all day with a client to make sure they were happy. But right now, I want nothing more than to hear Jillian's voice again.

I choke on Heather's perfume as she hugs my neck tightly. Glancing at my watch, I see it's getting late, and I'm positive Jillian has given up on me. It doesn't help that I have no idea where my phone is to see if she's contacted me. After stopping at the office to send the fax, I decide to drive to Jillian's instead of running to my brother's house. I knew she didn't live far from where the wedding took place, so when I google her name for an address, it isn't hard to locate the correct one.

She opens the door and her eyes widen in surprise. "What are you doing here?" As quickly as they'd risen, they fall into accusatory slits, accompanied by a hand on her hip for an extra spark of attitude. Her feistiness is incredibly sexy, though I wish that sometimes she would smile when she sees me instead of scowling.

"Can I come in?"

She rolls her eyes at my request, diminishing my confidence rapidly.

"Look, Sammy, I don't know what game you're playing, but I'm not in the mood."

I smack my hand against the door as she tries to slam it in my face. "After the kiss we shared, I wanted to see you. I haven't stopped thinking about you, Jillian. Please let me come in so we can talk."

"Don't you have enough kissing buddies?" Pinching her nose with her index finger and thumb, her now nasally voice adds, "I can smell her all over you."

"What you're smelling is the god-awful perfume of the female client I just met with." Cheap perfume mixed with a car air freshener I had rubbed on my clothes to mask the smell made for an interesting, but not at all pleasant, smell.

"Screwing a client? Seems like something you'd do."

I scoff. "You barely know me. What gives you the right to pretend you do?" Raising my voice at her hadn't been in my plan, but she just infuriates me so easily. Hopefully this fight ends in another kiss and not a kiss-off.

"You're right, I do barely know you. So let's just forget we ever met." Again, she attempts to slam the door on me, and I stop it with my hand once more. "What?" she exclaims.

"I *want* to know you."

Sharp tingles run through my fingers after striking the door repeatedly. I'm one slam away from having two sore hands. Even though I'm standing here in a small amount of discomfort, I still wish for her to invite me in.

"Why? All we do is fight." She looks as confused as I feel.

"I know. But for some reason, when I'm with you, I don't want to leave. And I want to know everything about you, including why I don't get mad when you call me Sammy." Only my mother has ever gotten away with it. Whenever anyone else calls me that stupid nickname, anger boils in my chest. But hearing it from Jillian's lips makes my body react much differently.

"I feel nothing but loathing for you." Her angry words are followed by the door slamming in my face, which I let happen this time. *What the hell did I do to her?*

For the half-hour drive to my brother's, I rack my brain for where things went wrong. When I open the door, I get an eyeful: my new sister-in-law is straddling my brother. For a moment, I stand there in shock, and then she spots me.

"Shit!" Carrie screams as she rushes to cover her breasts while falling off my brother on the couch. Turning around quickly, I cover my eyes and apologize repeatedly.

"Damn, bro. You're going to have to call or knock for a while."

"I'd have called, but I can't find my phone. Besides, you guys weren't supposed to be home for a few more days."

"We had to reschedule our cruise due to the hurricane coming in. It's expected right in the middle, so we took a voucher for a later one." Carrie returns, drowning in a T-shirt and shorts of Harrison's. "Have you been staying here since the wedding?"

"No, just since last night. My apartment building caught fire, and I have nowhere to stay. Do you mind if I crash here with you guys?"

Carrie covers her mouth with her hand and smacks Harrison, who's still sitting on the couch. "Tell your brother he's welcome to stay here." She pulls me in for a hug. "I'm glad you weren't hurt."

Harrison stands with a pillow in front of his junk, and I stare at the couch, noticing my phone on the cushion. "Oh, gross," I mutter with a cringe of disgust.

"I kept thinking we were hearing music," Carrie says matter-of-factly.

"What music?" I ask as I see no missed calls.

"I think it was 'Light My Fire' by the Doors." Fuck. That's the ringtone I chose for Jillian after finding out her occupation. "So you guys have been fucking with my phone underneath you and you answered it?"

"Dude, we didn't stop to answer your phone." My older brother is completely oblivious at times.

And now it all comes together. Jillian called me and they accidentally hit the Answer button, broadcasting their sex life to her. Making the obvious assumption, she thinks I was having sex with another woman.

"Thanks, big bro. I have to go save my potential love life now that I've interrupted yours." With index finger and thumb, I hold the tiniest edge of my phone as I try not to think about where it's been for the last few hours.

"I'll be back in a little while. I'll call first, once I disinfect my phone."

Thirty minutes in the car once more and I am back on Jillian's doorstep. I could've called, but I don't believe she'll answer. And there's the matter of my phone having ass germs. Definitely not putting that thing anywhere near my face, or touching it more than I absolutely have to.

The door swings open dramatically. The hand is back on her hip, her face practically screaming with annoyance. "What do you want, Sam?" Not even trying to irritate me anymore is a bad sign. Or maybe it's her way of letting me know she meant what she said earlier.

"My phone has been resting under Harrison's ass for the past two hours while he and Carrie had sex, and said ass answered the phone. They are the ones you heard screwing." No sense in spinning a tale in this case.

Her jaw drops open, and she steps aside, waving me in. "Ew. I could've gone my whole life without knowing that tidbit. I hope you cleaned your phone."

"I thought it would take more for you to believe me." I step just inside the door, taking up the space between Jillian and the exit. As long as I stand there, she can't slam the door on me—not easily, at least.

"If you were going to make up a lie, I would hope it would be less awkward and gross than that one."

My eyes drift to the ceiling as I consider her comment, and then I nod. There is no way I'd ever make something like that up.

"Can we start over? I'd love to take you out on a real date and let you see that I really am a nice guy." I can see her trying to think of a way out of it, the gears spinning behind her eyes. "Or we could start with coffee? Maybe now? I promised not to go home for the next few hours."

She cocks her eyebrow curiously. "Why?"

"I'm living with the newlyweds. Need I say more? Must I remind you they naked butt-dialed you."

Her face scrunches up and she shakes her head rapidly, probably trying to rid herself of that image. At least she didn't have to see it up close and personal.

She sighs and reaches behind the door. I hear keys jingling, which either means she's coming with me or she has a major padlock she's about to put on the door. Then again, it could mean she has mace on her key chain. I step back just in case it's the latter.

"Let's go." As she stops to lock the door, I use the opportunity to observe her backside. Her hair was always up when I'd seen her before, but now she has it down, and I see it reaches halfway to her round yet firm-looking ass. An ass framed perfectly in her jean shorts. Her black scoop-neck tee clings to her curvy body.

"I can feel you staring, but it's all right because my ass looks fantastic in these jeans." She's being facetious, it's obvious by the tone, but her words are true.

"Yes, it does," I murmur. She whips around with her mouth agape. "Um, you said it." I hold my hands up in the air, partly in surrender and so I can protect my face if she punches me.

"Thanks." The rosy hue on her cheeks is a good sign.

Going for coffee is tame compared to the dates I'm used

to. It seems so cliché that I never offer it. But Jillian needs to ease into this if she'll ever consider giving me a chance.

Frequently, I meet clients at a coffeehouse, one which happens to be only a few minutes from her house. Bringing people to a stuffy office isn't the first impression I want for everyone. Instead, Harrison and I arrange for them to meet us at the café and we buy them a drink and a snack to enjoy while we ask them about their dream homes. We find it relaxes them into a feeling of lunch with a friend instead of a business meeting. The closings are always done at the office though, for the more professional setting. And every once in a while, we get a client who insists we meet them at the office.

"Hey, Sam!" the barista greets me as I walk in. Immediately I receive the stink eye from Jillian, who most likely assumes I'm a player who brings girls here all the time.

The barista makes things worse by saying, "He's in here two, three times a week with someone new. He can read someone like a book, so he knows all the right things to say. He caffeinates them, sweetens them up, and moves on to the next one. It's fascinating."

Each second the annoyance on Jillian's face grows more apparent. Her lips form a thin line, and her eyes are glued to the exit sign, her body language explicitly stating she's ready to bolt.

Harper, the barista, pales. "I didn't mean it in a bad way."

"My friend Jillian here doesn't realize you're talking about my real estate clients, so you're making me sound like a man whore, Harper. Hence the look on her face, because this is a date." Today is not my day for winning points with this woman. Everyone is against me.

"Not a date," Jillian corrects me immediately.

Harper mouths, "Ouch, sorry," and finishes taking our orders.

"I thought we were starting fresh?" I ask Jillian as we wait for our drinks. Could she be having second thoughts already?

"We are, and I like to get to know someone before I date them."

Her logic befuddles me.

"Dating is about getting to know someone, isn't it?"

"Dating is about hand-holding and kissing. Having sex," Jillian clarifies.

"Exactly, so let's do all of that," I say with a wink, hoping to lighten the mood. Instead, she rolls her eyes at me, but when she turns her head away, I see a glimpse of a smile. She isn't making things easy for me, and I love a challenge.

With my palm against her cheek, I turn her face toward me. "Just breaking the ice." As her name is called to grab her drink, I mumble, "And boy is it icy in here."

Jillian returns with her caramel macchiato cappuccino topped with foam and cinnamon sprinkles shaped into a heart. Before I can make a comment about the romantic appearance, she sticks her finger straight through the heart and swirls it around, removing the shape entirely.

"Isn't that hot?"

"I work in a firehouse. This is nothing."

Knocking a brick wall down with my bare fists would be less challenging than getting this woman to smile at me. "Who built those walls?"

"What walls?" She glances around the room as if I'm being literal.

"The ones around your heart." Sure, it's a cheesy line, but her eyes soften, and I see the slight hint of a smile curve her lips. My goal is to get a full smile out of her before the end of this… well, whatever we're calling it.

"Long story." Two words people use too often to mean they don't want to talk about it, or the blunt meaning is "It's none of your business."

Being a regular, Harper knows I tip well, so she delivers my smoothie personally. I thank her whilst slipping her a ten and return my attention to the challenge in front of me.

"Jillian, I like you."

Her defenses flare up. "Why?"

It's a question I've been asking myself as I struggle and wear myself out to get so much as pleasant conversation from her. I choose to put it more delicately.

"I honestly don't know. It's a feeling I get when I'm around you. A sense of calm, a familiarity. Even when you push me away or shut me out, I want to push back." Looking away from her, I nervously mutter, "You're like a drug for me."

I watch as her hand slides across the table until it lays on top of mine. "We might need to get you into rehab." And then she tosses her head back and lets out a genuine laugh. The smile meets her eyes and softens her stern appearance.

She's worn such a hard expression on her face since the moment we met; seeing her let loose is what I've been waiting for.

One win for me today.

"I want to apologize. I haven't given you a proper chance to get to know me. And I'm not afraid to admit I'm curious about you myself." Her apology comes unexpectedly as I'm taking a drink of my smoothie.

I choke a bit in surprise.

I can't figure this woman out. She runs so hot and cold it makes my head spin trying to keep up. Infuriating, yet exhilarating at the same time.

She smiles. "Let's get out of here and do something I choose. If you stick with me on it, I'll agree to go on a proper date with you. If not, well then, we can part as acquaintances."

I'm nervous, but curious about her suggestion.

She stands first and towers over me in my seated position. I'll admit, she's a bit intimidating. Her long arm reaches toward me, and I shake her hand, hoping I haven't agreed to do something completely insane.

One thing I know is there's a small hole in that wall now. It may be just a drain, but something is getting through, and that's what matters to me.

"Mind telling me where we're going? Since I'm driving and all," I ask as I hold the door for her. When she steps outside, she spins around and smiles, continuing to walk backward.

"Let me drive?" It isn't a demand, it's a request.

Glancing over at my fairly new, "never been driven by anyone but me, I call her baby and never put her in a corner" cherry-red Jeep Wrangler, I sigh and hold my hand out. Relinquishing the keys, I trudge behind her, saying a silent prayer that she won't wreck the love of my life—or my heart, for that matter.

CHAPTER EIGHT

JILLIAN

"Breathe, Sammy. It's just a car." When I asked him to let me drive, you'd think I'd asked him to chop a baby in half. I watch him go through fear, reluctance, and eventually defeat in a matter of seconds. If he had said no, I'd have still gone out with him, but this is more fun. Sadly, I enjoy giving him a hard time way too much. We're still sitting in the lot of the coffeehouse. I swear his face has turned a shade of blue from lack of oxygen.

"Geez, Sam, if it's that a big a deal, you can drive."

My eyes follow his gaze to see if I'm missing something. Ahead of us, a man and a woman are standing close, having a rather intimate-looking conversation. I don't recognize either of them. "Do you know them?"

The spell lifts, and he shakes his head. "No, but I thought maybe…. Anyway, let's go. Just be gentle." As we pull out of the parking lot, I notice his eyes follow the couple until they're out of his sight range. Something in his eyes tells me he knows them but isn't ready to talk about it. I can relate to that, so I don't push further.

"Mind if we stop and pick up a few things really quick?"

He shrugs, staring out the window. *What's ruined his mood so quickly?* Hopefully what I have in mind will cheer him up.

He asks no questions as I run inside the store where everything's a dollar and come back with ten bags of goodies. The rest of the ride is quiet up until we reach the hospital. "What are we doing here?"

"Cheering *you* up now, it seems."

"Sorry, Jillian, I didn't mean to be so quiet. I lied before." As he fidgets nervously, I wait patiently for him to find the words. It takes him a moment to gather his thoughts before elaborating. "The woman in the lot was someone I proposed to once. Her name is Anya. She told me she never wanted to be tied down to anyone." From the sound of it, Sam had been attached to someone who treated him as crappy as my last relationship.

"Guess she's tied down now. That bump looked to be about six months along." A terrible thought enters my mind at how this drama may unfold. "Um… is it possible it's yours?"

"No. We did accidentally get pregnant while together.

We've been apart for two years now. She had an abortion because she never wanted to be a mom either. Guess it was just me she didn't want all of that with." He's laying out his vulnerability like a tablecloth in front of me.

"You're still in love with her?" The question spills forth before I can stop myself, but I don't want to know the answer because it can possibly end whatever this is before it truly starts.

"No, I'm not. Don't know if I ever really was in love with her in the first place. Being lied to about something so big hurts though. Plus, I love kids. When she had the abortion, it almost destroyed me."

Sarcasm and a sense of humor are some of my favorite things about Sam so far. Seeing him sitting here with his heart on his sleeve is difficult to witness.

"We could do this another day. I'm not sure it's what you need after hearing the story of your past."

When I have a day off and a little money in the bank, I spend the afternoon at the hospital in town visiting patients. As a first responder, I know some of the burn victims personally. Children are especially concerning, but I don't limit myself to just the young ones—everyone needs to feel loved. The hospital has some limits, but they give me a little leeway when it comes to putting things on the walls.

"I bought some toys and decorations and candy to share with the patients. There are a lot of children inside, and I don't want it to make you sad." Sad*der* is probably the more appropriate word. Practically downtrodden by seeing his ex. No matter how nasty the breakup, I know from experience how seeing them again can stab.

"No. That's… wow. You voluntarily come spend hours with people you don't know?" His eyes scrunch up, and he scowls. "Sorry, I wasn't trying to sound conceited or anything. I think it's amazing." He smiles, and it seems genuine. "Let's do this. Show me what you do."

As we walk in, I move toward Sam, wanting to reach out to him, but he shoves his hands in his pockets. Interpreting the move as rejection, it hurts my assurance of where this is going between us.

"Hey, gorgeous!" Adam spots me as we cross through the Emergency waiting area. He gives me a kiss on the cheek and grins. "I'm Adam, and you are?"

"Sam. How do you two know each other?" I know Adam well enough to know he'll enjoy making Sam squirm a bit. We're a lot alike in that regard. And I have to confess, the shade of green on his face right now is kind of hot.

Adam leans forward to whisper, "I'm married… to a guy."

To which Sam's shoulders relax and a smile appears on his face. "Nice to meet you."

"I thought it might be." Adam winks and turns to me. "Here for the rounds?"

"Yep. Can you show us where to start?"

Adam and the nurses keep tabs on who gets the least visitors so volunteers like me can give them a little love first. The other guys in my crew also spend a day off or two here when they can. Many have families or loved ones keeping them busy, but the single ones make it happen regularly.

Even if I'm not single one day, I plan to have my significant other come with me instead of limiting my days. Bringing Sam here is my way of seeing how he handles it. Dipping toes in the water, so to speak.

"We have a special one today who needs you. She was in a car accident, and her parents have been sedated ever since because of their injuries. She came in last night and has no other family. Only five years old. Her name is Mikayla. We've been doing our best to keep her company, but you know how busy it gets." Quietly, he waves us to follow him and points her out through the window in the door.

Sam grabs the bags from my hand. "What do you have in here?" After he rifles through the bags a moment, he looks up at Adam. "Do you have a gift shop?"

"Down the hall to the right. Remember it's room 106. Just have me paged if you need me." A nurse calls Adam away to see a patient, so I let Sam lead the way.

Following him blindly to the gift shop, I admit I'm a little offended. "Why are we buying more stuff? I know it doesn't look like much, but kids love stickers and coloring."

"I know. What you have is great, but I just wanted to get one more thing." In the gift shop, he heads straight for the pile of stuffed animals. He stares at them for about a minute before picking up a chubby penguin.

"Stuffed penguin?"

"She's five, and her parents aren't sitting next to her bed. She needs protection."

The moment we exit the gift shop, he reaches for me. Without further explanation, he escorts me down the hallway toward the room number Adam gave us. Once he grabs my hand, the rest of the walk is a blur. All I can focus on is the heat of his hand, the soft feel of his skin against mine, the gentle way his thumb strokes my skin. I want to say something to him, but the words don't form. I stare at his face, the light stubble along his jaw. At the wedding he'd been clean-shaven. While still incredibly attractive, I like the scruffy look on him even better.

"Excuse me, miss?" he says to the little girl lying in bed, trembling at the sight of strangers. "Are you"—He holds the penguin up to his ear for a listen. "—Mikayla?"

The dark-eyed beauty with her hair full of braids peers her big eyes up at Sam and answers, "Yes."

Pressing the penguin against his ear again, he murmurs, "I'm getting to it. Give me a minute." Rolling his eyes, he turns back to Mikayla. "Penny—" Again the penguin presses to his ear. "—oops, sorry. *Percy* claims—" Back to the ear, and Sam feigns annoyance. "Dude, let me finish a sentence."

The little girl laughs as I wonder if he's lost every marble in his head.

"As I was saying, before Percy so rudely interrupted me." Percy the penguin now looks across the room, away from Sam. "He says he was sent here to be your protector. Would you be so kind as to let him stay in your room and watch over things?"

Mikayla nods and reaches out for Percy. She gives him a long squeeze and whispers, "He's soft and fat."

A cartoon voice rings out from nearby. "I prefer chubby, madam." She giggles, and the voice continues. "Percy P.

Penguin at your service. I do enjoy hugs, by the way." Sam is providing the voice, though I can barely tell by the smile on his face. Each time we're together, he surprises me. How do I compete with ventriloquism?

"What's your name?" Mikayla asks.

"Percy...."

She giggles and clarifies, "No, Percy. The man who brought you to me."

"Sam. And this beauty beside me is my friend Jillian. We were hoping, if Percy's approval is met, that we could sit and color with you, or maybe put stickers on things we shouldn't. Like the walls and chairs?"

The possibility of falling in love with this man just rose to the highest percentage. Even Mikayla seems to be swooning from his charm.

"Ahem." Percy clears his throat. "There will be no tomfoolery in here."

"Tomfoolery? Percy must be the oldest penguin in the world!" I say, unable to control the jab at Sam.

Keeping in character, he has Percy grunt his disapproval.

"What is tom food larry?" Mikayla scrunches her face in confusion.

"It means we can't put stuff on the walls. But I have coloring books with superheroes and princesses. Which would you prefer?" I reach into the bag, expecting a typical girl response of princesses when I'm pleasantly surprised that she wants superheroes instead.

"I love superheroes too."

And for the next hour, I watch Sam let Mikayla pick

out the colors for the outfits and explain to him the stories behind some of the characters. In one evening, I go from being completely annoyed with the man to practically in love with him. He's so gentle and patient with her, and it's endearing.

We spend two hours with Mikayla, and then for the next two to three hours, we walk the halls visiting with people. One of the older women we meet flirts shamelessly with Sam. Instead of letting her down easy, he flirts back, leaving her with a huge grin on her face even though she has burns on most of her body. For a little while, he helps her forget about the pain. Before we say goodbye, he gives her a kiss on the cheek and promises he'll come back to see her again.

By the time we finish, I'm starving. "Are you hungry?"

"I can eat. Where would you like to go?" He reaches for my hand again as we walk to the car. He takes it so easily, as if it's second nature for us to hold hands. We're already falling into a routine, and I don't want this feeling to end.

I tug on his hand to stop him. "What's wrong?" he asks.

Swiping my tongue quickly across my lips, I lean in and kiss him before I lose my nerve to be assertive. He pushes my hair behind my ear with his fingertips while I suck on his bottom lip.

"I'm assuming this is a date now?"

"I have the ingredients for a homemade pizza, if you're good with it." His eyes sparkle as I suggest my place. "Don't get any ideas. I'm only offering pizza."

"Sounds perfect."

To my surprise, he offers to let me drive the car back

to my house. He even lets me choose the tunes on the radio. Noticing an iPod attached to the stereo, I start up his playlist. The first song is "Dragula" by Rob Zombie. "You like Zombie?"

"Yeah. Saw him twice at Bridgestone Arena in Nashville. Once it was with Alice Cooper and the other time with Korn. The man puts on an amazing show. And not to brag, but I touched his arm when he came down off the stage."

"I was at the Cooper show! Did you dress up?" The show was Halloween weekend that year and most people wore costumes. "My friend Stephan got tickets, and we went dressed as the grim reaper and a sexy nurse."

"Really? Do you still have the sexy nurse outfit?"

"Stephan was dressed as the sexy nurse. I was the grim reaper." After a brief show of disappointment, Sam laughs. "If I can find the pictures of us, you'll laugh even more. Stephan didn't shave his legs or face, so his costume involved a short skirt and halter top displaying a hairy chest, legs, and full beard. He kept his facial hair cut close normally, but when we bought the tickets, he came up with the outfit and grew it out. From the back with his wig on, from the waist up at least, you would've thought he was a hot chick. And then he'd turn around and scare everyone half to death."

"Stephan sounds like a fun guy."

"He is. He lives right there." I point at the house next door after parking the car.

"He's your neighbor?" Jealousy colors his features once more. "Did you ever date?"

"Nope. I'm not his type." Beyond the fear of settling down, Stephan doesn't actually have a type, other than female. He doesn't discriminate on size, color, intelligence level—if he's attracted to her, he'll bring her home. He's always honest with them too. They know he isn't relationship material, and they don't care. Win-win for everyone involved.

"Oh, he's gay too?" Sam asks, eyeing the house.

"No. But he's told me I'm too good for him. His words, not mine."

"You disagree with him?" Following me into the house, he isn't letting the issue drop quickly. He doesn't seem to be satisfied with a simple "no," so I spell it out for him.

"He's a player. A great friend, a stud, and a gentleman, but still a commitment-phobe. I want something more stable. I don't consider myself better than him though." I set my keys in the bowl next to the door and lock it behind Sam. "The kitchen is this way." I pull a pan out from under the stove and set it on the island. "Dough, peppers, and cheese are in the fridge. I'll get the sauce and pepperoni out of the pantry."

He grabs the roll of dough from the fridge and together we smear on pizza sauce, fresh peppers, and shredded cheese, topping it off with two layers of pepperoni.

We pop it in the oven, and twenty minutes later we have a beautiful steaming cheesy pie. Using a pot holder, I pull it out of the oven. Sam found the pizza cutter with no problem; he's quickly becoming accustomed with my kitchen arrangement.

Each grabbing two slices, we sit down at the table to eat. Instead of sitting across from me, he chooses the seat next to mine. Eating in front of a guy has never bothered me, so I eagerly bite into the slice, licking my lips to gather any stray sauce or cheese after.

"You have something…." He leans forward with a napkin as though he's going to wipe my mouth, and then he kisses me instead. I can taste the bit of sauce on his tongue, moaning when his hands come to rest on my thighs. He scoots forward in his chair, his leg moving between mine and bringing us closer.

"Oops," I mumble against his lips. "I got sauce on your shirt."

"I'll just take it off and we can wash it." He removes his shirt, exposing ridged muscles and washboard abs. I suck my bottom lip between my teeth and release a sigh of admiration. He smirks in response, obviously enjoying my appreciation of his body. Running my fingers along his taut abs, I can't believe I'm being so bold with him. I trace the dark brown line of hair from his belly button to the waistband of his pants before I dip my finger in and pop the button open.

My brain is screaming to stop touching him, but my hands have a mind of their own. And feeling his chest, the warmth it causes between my legs, and the ache for more of him, I need my hands to disobey my brain.

Running his finger across the slice on his plate, he pulls some sauce off the edge and smears it across my shirt. "Oops, look like you have to remove yours now too. Wouldn't want it to stain."

Damn, he's good.

I waste no time standing up, pulling my shirt off and tossing it away from me. After it lands across the room, I turn back to see lust-filled eyes staring at my body.

Now standing face-to-face, the heat in the room has risen at least ten degrees. His fingertip slides under my bra strap as he pulls it off my shoulder. Leaving a trail of kisses across my collarbone and down over the swell of my breasts, his lips stay in contact with my skin, never once relenting. Moving his hands around my waist and up my back, I feel the release as they find the clasp to my bra. Gently he glides my bra down and off my arms until it falls to the floor.

I bite my lip as Sam stands back a moment to let his eyes drift over my naked form, at least from the waist up. He sucks in a breath as I unbutton my shorts and shimmy them down my legs. I step out of them, standing in front of him in nothing but panties.

He grins and lets out a short chuckle. I peer down and realize I hadn't been prepared for a date when I dressed this morning. My panties are covered with penguins wearing scarves.

And to make the humiliation stronger, I snort, to which Sam laughs again. He reaches forward, cupping my cheeks in his hands, and says, "You're adorable as hell. Do you have any idea? I've never met anyone like you, Jillian,"

"Why do you call me Jillian?"

"Do you want me to stop?"

"No, I don't want you to stop anything. As much as I've

tried to deny my attraction to you, the truth is I've thought about you nonstop since the moment I saw you on that sidewalk."

Sam cringes, most likely embarrassed by the memory.

"So, do I have to spill sauce on your pants to get you to take them off too?"

In response, Sam reaches down and places my hands on his belt. "No, but you can help me take them off."

He doesn't have to ask me twice. I fumble with the buckle as our lips crash together in a frenzy. As I work on his zipper, he pushes my panties over my ass and lets them fall to the ground. We take a step to the side, freeing ourselves from the last vestiges of clothing, and then Sam lifts me, my legs wrapping around his waist of their own accord. Warmth pools between my thighs, anxious to have him inside me. Rational thinking is almost impossible.

Laying me down on the couch, he hovers above me.

"Please tell me you have something?" I whisper to Sam as I feel his erection pressing against my stomach.

He groans against my ear. "I was hoping you did."

And the moment ends as quickly as it began.

Sam rolls off me and onto the floor, his flagpole mocking me.

"Give me two minutes. Don't move."

I pull my raincoat from the closet and tie it shut.

Grabbing my spare key, just in case, I run next door to Stephan's house. He has girls in and out of his house at least monthly, sometimes more frequently when he isn't traveling for business, so I know he's always prepared

"Hey, Jilli. What's up, honey?" He eyes my apparel, pops his head outside, and looks up at the sky. "Is it supposed to rain?"

Ignoring his question, I say, "I need to borrow something."

"Exotic spice?" Stephan asks. A question he poses every time I come over now since he still has a cabinet full of them.

"Condom." Stephan gasps, covers his mouth and pulls me into his arms. "What are you doing?"

"I've been waiting on this day for so long. You're about to be a woman again."

"I'm not a virgin, dumbass." I shove him away from me.

"Hence the *again*, dumbass." He turns to the right, reaches in a drawer next to the door, and pulls out a string of condoms. "Wait, are you naked under there?" He tries to pull at my coat, and I smack his hand away. "Damn, girl, I'm so proud. One or two?"

Glancing at the roll of eight or ten at least, I grab the entire set. "That should do it."

As I run back toward my house, he howls in my direction.

"I'm back!" I yell as I burst back through my front door. Lying on the couch, still at full attention, is the most beautiful specimen of a man I've ever laid eyes on. For a moment, I enjoy the scenery splayed out in front of me. Then I swallow back the terror rising in my throat. It's been so long since I've had sex that I wonder if my skills are up to par.

What if I'm not good? Will he run away, screaming about the bad sex he just had?

Sam struts over and takes the condoms from my hand. He's over six feet and all muscle, yet light-footed, like a cat on the prowl. Tearing one open, he throws the rest to the chair next to him. After gliding the condom over his erection, he begins a trail of kisses along my neck. "This raincoat is going to star in future fantasies of mine with you."

"You've fantasized about me?"

"Since the night we met."

Earlier we had been ready and raring to go, but now he's taking things slow, and I have to say I'm enjoying the new pace. I'll soon find out if I'm still good at it—wild horses can't stop me now.

He unties the coat, slips it off my shoulders, and kisses a path down the length of my body. Taking a knee in front of me, he lifts my leg over his shoulder and nibbles his way across my thigh. Tiny, delicate, mind-blowing nibbles until just before he reaches my center. Warm air coats my skin as he exhales, followed by one pleasurable but torturous lick of my core, his breath sending a warm tingle from my head to my toes. The moment his tongue goes back in, the sensation almost knocks me completely off my feet.

To keep me steady, Sam reaches around to cup my ass, simultaneously holding me up and pushing his tongue deeper. When the first quiver of an orgasm hits, I try to pull away from the intensity, but he's stronger and keeps me grounded, holding me close as he finishes me off.

When I open my eyes, his face is in front of mine, his eyes glowing with passion and lust. Our lips meet, my flavor still lingering on his tongue. No man has made me come from oral sex before, and kissing someone after always seemed weird to me, but with Sam it's erotic. I can't kiss him enough. Like a bowl of creamy dark chocolate gelato with peanut butter cups, I crave him. His taste is my addiction, and I want—*need*—more.

Our arms tangle together while our feet guide us back toward the wall. He raises me higher, and I close my legs around him and gasp as he enters me. Each thrust goes deeper than the last, and it's as though I'm trying to climb the wall behind me to take in more of him. Our eyes focus on each other with such intensity, the pleasure unreal, almost dreamlike.

If I am dreaming, I'll kill anyone who wakes me up.

He grunts as I dig my nails into his back. Our moans become louder as I beg him not to stop. A surge of ecstasy lifts me up. As my body quivers with climax, I close my eyes and grip his shoulders tighter, prolonging the rush. I bite my lip as our eyes meet once more. His dark, lustful gaze makes me tighten my legs around him. With a final thrust, he throws his head back as he growls his release.

After we catch our breath, he lets me down and continues nibbling on my skin, this time around my ear. "Round two?" he asks just before tugging on my earlobe with his teeth.

I'm not even close to done with him tonight.

"Grab the condoms and follow me," I command.

He obeys well as we literally run to my bedroom. Stopping at the door, he removes the used condom and tosses it in the wastebasket. I'm waiting for him by the bed, and as he struts toward me, I wet my lips. With a gentle shove, I push him down on the bed and straddle his waist.

Sitting back, this time I take the condom and glide it over him, taking my time, covering every inch. Moving forward, I hover above him, lowering myself while slowly taking pleasure in having him inside me again. His soft hands cup my breasts, massaging gently yet firmly as I buck against him.

The ride is long and steady as I take my time, enjoying the feel of him sliding in and out.

Unable to look at him for fear of the intense moment from before, I close my eyes and match moans with Sam. We seem to be trying to outdo each other's ecstasy; starting with soft sighs, we advance to screams of pleasure, mixing them with dirty phrases. He begs me to go faster, and when I can't reach his desired pace, he flips me over and grabs onto the bedpost. Pumping harder, he screams my name and I shudder beneath him, tightening my legs around his waist to keep him pressing against me for the most intense release.

Third time is the charm for me tonight. We collapse against the bed, both sweaty and pleased in unmeasurable ways. I turn on my side, not sure what to do now. My boyfriend before usually got up to shower and then watch television. I want to curl up against his skin, to keep the closeness between us, but I wait for Sam to make the move.

Sam lies behind me, plants a kiss against my shoulder, and places his hand on my hip. "I hope it's okay if I stay over. I don't think I could walk after tonight."

"It's more than okay."

With permission granted for his sleepover, he drapes his arm across my stomach, his breath caressing my neck as he quickly falls asleep. Lying there in his arms is comfortable, safe—like home, as though it's right where I'm meant to be.

Everything about him is adorable, even the way he snores softly. And the longer I lie there thinking about him, the tighter the fear grips my chest. I'm falling hard and fast, and it terrifies me. I'm envisioning waking up like this every day, even the possibility of kids. After seeing him with Mikayla, I couldn't imagine a better dad.

Closing my eyes, I try to sleep, my thoughts getting too carried away for something so new.

Light pours in through my windows, waking me from the peaceful sleep I finally fell into around two in the morning. A little after seven, according to the clock, I roll over to find the other side of the bed empty.

He may have slipped out once I fell asleep to avoid talking about what happened with us. Even if I never see him again, at least I had one night of perfect, amazing sex, one night where someone made me feel like the most beautiful woman in the world. I stretch my arms above my head and smile at the memory of last night.

"Damn. I was hoping to get in here and wake you up myself." Sam strolls in, wearing my *Star Wars* apron and carrying a tray of food. My smile grows wider knowing he's still here.

"Are you serving me breakfast naked?"

He turns to reveal his firm, beautiful naked ass. Setting the tray on my lap, he leans over and places the most tender kiss against my lips.

"Would you rather I wear clothes?"

"No," I reply, barely letting him finish his question. "I've never been served breakfast in bed, especially by someone wearing my favorite apron."

"Is this an old boyfriend's apron?"

"Are you kidding?" I don't need to feign offense—I am genuinely offended. "I sat in line overnight to get tickets to *Rogue One* last year. If you can't handle me being a *Star Wars* fanatic, and an all-around nerd, you—" I stop when he kneels on the floor. "What are you doing?"

"Marry me." His face shows no signs of joking around.

My heart skips a beat, wondering if I should run for my life from this crazy person or say yes and enjoy the hot sex for as long as possible.

"Breathe, Jillian. I'm only half serious." *Half serious?* "Do you know how long I've looked for a woman who loves those movies as much as I do?"

"Want to see something possibly frightening to you?"

He snorts, and it's likely I love him for it. "How does one possibly answer a question like that?" Holding his hand out, he says, "Let's go see it."

"Follow me." Setting the tray on the nightstand, I take his hand and lead him to the spare bedroom in my house. When I open the door, he gasps in shock and ventures inside.

"Holy mother of…." His eyes widen as he takes in the sight before him. "I might be 100 percent serious about the proposal after all."

As a teen, I was goth on the outside but a nerd on the inside. I covered my lack of confidence in a black shroud, and my home was my place of worship. I began collecting everything from autographs to action figures, and even statues. A life-size statue of Darth Vader fills one corner, a stormtrooper occupies another, and there's a life-size Yoda on the nightstand. It isn't all just *Star Wars* though. Along the way I've collected superhero memorabilia, and even the occasional Barbie, though granted there are always special editions such as the *X-Files* set of Scully and Mulder.

"Not freaked out?" I ask timidly.

"More like turned on. Is it strange that I want to have sex in this room with Darth Vader watching?"

"Um…." In all honesty, the thought has crossed my mind before as well. Our freaky natures match—another plus to how this could all turn out. I still don't want to admit it so soon though.

"Kidding. It's really more about Yoda." He turns and throws me a wink. If he never comes over again, at least I'll always have the view of him in my apron. "Breakfast is getting cold. Let's go eat, and then I want to fully explore this room."

He starts down the hall, heading back to my bedroom, and I enjoy the scenery along the way as I follow. *Hate to see you go, but love to watch you walk away. It should be a crime to have an ass so perfect.*

"I can feel you staring, but it's all right because my ass looks fantastic in nothing at all."

He's using my own line on me, so I give him back his response of "Yes it does."

I finally see the tray's contents: bacon, eggs, toast, a bowl of strawberries, and a dollop of whipped cream. Seems he thought of everything. "I didn't realize I had all this in my refrigerator. I haven't been grocery shopping this week."

"You had the eggs and bread. I went for a run this morning and grabbed some things on my way back. I wanted to make this morning special. I'm glad you slept so hard. I was afraid you'd wake up and think I slipped out on you." He bites into a crisp slice of bacon and lets it hang from his lips. Moving closer, I bite down on the other end. We meet in the middle and our lips touch briefly before his tongue slips past my lips. "Best bacon I've ever tasted," he whispers against my mouth.

I reach for a strawberry and run it through the whipped cream. Slowly dragging it across his lips, I try to be seductive, but then just before leaning in, I smear the whipped cream across his face. He sputters a curse and then laughs. Pushing me down on the bed, I squeal as he attempts to kiss me, trying to pull away, but I just end up with whipped cream all over my face.

"Sit still," he demands. His mouth moves to my cheek, lapping up the cream. When he drags his tongue across my bottom lip, I suck in air as his fingers dance across my thighs.

"Don't you work today?" I gasp out as he trails closer to my sweet spot.

"I work for myself. And if clients need me, they can call.

I have more important things to take care of today."

No need to tell me twice. Who am I to argue with a man who knows what he wants?

His fingers dip inside me, and I moan his name. "Sammy." It comes out of my mouth from habit, but he doesn't seem to mind. Instead, he moves faster and groans against my ear.

"Condom."

And an hour later, I'm asleep in his arms once more.

CHAPTER
NINE

My time with Jillian is interrupted around noon. I'd been perfectly content lying here with my arms around her naked body when my phone started ringing. I grab it quickly, trying not to wake her. As quiet as I'm trying to be, I realize she's awake when her arms move around my chest and she kisses my back. "Who was it?"

Rolling over, I kiss her before answering. "Client. I hate to do this, but I need to go. If you don't mind, I'd like to come back here this evening and see you. I don't have to stay, but…."

"You could stay if you want." Her answer is exactly what I was hoping for. Not pushing me away or throwing up her walls again is a good sign. "I mean… it's up to you."

"Don't do that. Don't backtrack. I'm here with you, Jillian, which is exactly where I want to be. Don't talk yourself out of this happening between us. Promise me?"

"I promise." Green eyes stare up at me, so trusting and genuine. No way in hell will I let this woman push me away again. She may have been a challenge in the beginning that I had to overcome, but now I'm a goner. Falling hard, fast, and deep into love with this woman hadn't been the plan, but it's the road I'm currently heading down. And I don't think it will be a long road.

Jillian watches me dress. Feeling her eyes on me is making it harder for me to leave. On the bed, sitting up with the sheet pressed against her naked form, the light dancing off her skin, she's a beautiful sight, one I could get used to seeing every day.

Crawling across the bed, I kiss her. "If you want to stay exactly like this until I get back, I'd be good with it."

She giggles. "I bet you would. Go meet your client, and I'll see you tonight. I'll have dinner ready when you get home."

Her referring to her house as my home gives me the warm and fuzzies. I love it even more when she doesn't rephrase it after.

"I left a beautiful naked woman in bed to come here and meet this client. Where are they?"

Harrison told me we had a client needing to meet as

soon as possible. We've been sitting at the office for an hour waiting on them to arrive, and I'm growing impatient. Actually, I'm past impatient at this point. All I want to do is go back to Jillian's and be with her.

"Let me call them again. All I know is Carrie took the message and said the client is desperate to meet with us. They're in a pinch and need a house in town with a budget of half a million. I couldn't pass it up. While we wait, you could tell me about this naked woman." Harrison is always the first to hear about my conquests since, in the past, I've needed to vent and complain about the majority.

"Not this time."

Slack-jawed with surprise, he finally replies, "Wow, really?"

With Jillian, I have no complaints, and I care too much about her to share intimate details of our sex life. I regretted saying the naked part as soon as it came out of my mouth, knowing it would lead to this line of questioning.

"You'll meet her soon enough. She's different… special. I want to enjoy it for a while before I end up screwing it up like I've done with every other relationship."

The doorbell to the office alerts us to someone walking in. A moment later, the receptionist, Daphne, enters the room.

"Your client has arrived. Should I let him in?"

"Please," I state. "And can you find out what he would like to drink and bring that in as well? Harrison and I will take waters."

Daphne leaves, Harrison follows her to greet the man,

and I stew over how long this has already taken. When the client steps in the room, my mind goes completely blank on everything else. The man who walks in is the one who'd been speaking to Anya in the parking lot the other day.

"Garth Howard." The man extends his hand to me.

Harrison glares at me curiously when I'm reluctant to shake at first. I quickly cover by wiping my hand on my pants. "Sorry, sweaty palms." I shake his hand. "Sam Warner. How can we help you?"

"Well, my wife and I are looking for a new place and we need it quick. I was recently transferred here by my company. We've been living in a hotel room, and she's threatened divorce if I don't get us a stable house soon." He chuckles, and Harrison joins him. I just stare blankly. "Anyway, my budget is half a million. I prefer something in the Brentwood area if possible, but she has very precise taste."

Grabbing a sheet of paper, Harrison asks the usual questions of square footage, number of bedrooms, baths, yard size, etcetera. When he finishes, I turned to Garth and casually ask, "Four bedrooms? Big family?"

"No, no kids, and no plans for kids. We like the extra space so we can each have an office and a spare bedroom. If you can find one with an apartment outside over a garage, that would be helpful too. For guests, I mean."

No plans for kids? Maybe Anya is giving the baby up for adoption.

"How long have you been married?" Harrison peers at me curiously when I ask a question not on the usual list.

"Fourteen years," he responds.

To which I boldly reply, "What the fuck?"

Water spews from Harrison's lips when he hears my statement slash question.

"Excuse me?" Mr. Howard bellows.

"How old was she when you got married, fifteen?" I stand up, enraged at the thought that I'd been lied to either about Anya's age or marital status. Although neither lie will be easier to handle.

"Not sure why it matters, but we were both twenty." Switching from me to Harrison, he waves his hands in the air. "I'm sorry, is there something I'm missing here?"

"I'm wondering that myself," Harrison quips.

"I know Anya," I deadpan.

The look on Garth's face is a mixture of surprise and horror. He straightens his tie and swallows. "How—I mean, who is Anya?"

"Your wife?"

"My wife's name is Vanessa. You must have me mistaken with someone else."

"I saw you. In the parking lot yesterday. It was obvious that you knew each other on a personal level. If she's not your wife, why did the two of you look so chummy?"

Harrison sits dumbfounded. He stares at the two of us, our nostrils flaring as we ready to fight.

"How do you know Anya?" His tone is accusatory, as though *I'm* the one with something to hide.

"Ex-girlfriend. We broke up two years ago. Does your wife know about her?"

Garth stands up and turns toward the door. "I believe I need a different agency," he throws over his shoulder before leaving the room.

Harrison rushes to follow him. A few minutes later, he comes back in with steam pouring from his ears. "I hope you're happy. You lost a huge commission with that guy. Why do you care if he's cheating on his wife, even if it is Anya? She treated you like crap."

"She's pregnant, Harrison."

And those three words clear everything up for him. He's the one who let me cry on his shoulder without judgment when Anya aborted our baby. When she walked out on me, he let me crash on his couch until I found a new place to live without memories of her. And now he'll be here for me through this.

"Shit, man. Although, I gotta say it's sort of karma. I mean, she never wanted to be a parent, took the choice completely away from you, and now she's stuck raising a kid completely on her own. Based on her character, I would be willing to bet that she kept the kid hoping it would make him leave his wife."

"I'm sorry about losing the client. I wasn't expecting it to be him walking in here. It threw me for a loop."

Patting my shoulder, Harrison sighs, and I know he understands.

"Get out of here, man. Go see your mystery lady and forget about Anya."

My intentions when I leave are to do exactly what he suggests. Instead, I find myself sitting outside of Anya's apartment complex.

We haven't spoken since the breakup, so it's highly possible that she doesn't live here anymore, but I take the chance and knock. She answers the door in a tank top, her pregnant belly sticking out, and a pair of yoga pants.

"Sam?" Shock is, without a doubt, the best way to describe her reaction to seeing me. "What are you…?" She pauses and places her hand against her stomach before looking away in apparent shame.

"Hello, Anya. You look…."

"Pregnant?" she tries to joke, but neither of us laughs. Holding the door open wider, she invites me inside. "What brings you by?"

"I saw you the yesterday."

"You did? Where?" She clears a spot on the couch, moving blankets and a pillow to let me sit down. "Sorry, I haven't slept well lately, so I've been watching television until I crash on the couch."

"Noproblem.Youwereoutsidethecafétalkingtosomeone."

"Oh." Running her hand along her belly, she looks away from me once more. "He's the father. It's complicated."

"I know." Her head whips around, though her eyes are still not on me. "He came into the agency looking for a house for him and his wife, who I thought was you."

Tears stream down her face as she starts to sob. I've never seen Anya show so much emotion—ever. The day of the abortion, she was completely stone-faced, as though she were having a normal routine procedure.

When I make the mistake of reaching out to pat her

shoulder, she takes it as an invitation and throws her arms around me. Sobbing against my ear, she presses closer to me, and I cringe. "He's never going to leave her. He told me he would, but now he's looking for a house?"

"Did you keep the baby so he would leave her?" She didn't have to answer, the look on her face speaking volumes. "So, if I'd been married and cheating on my wife, you'd have kept our baby?" Her sobs grow louder, and she clings to me once more. I wonder if it's an act or if she's truly regretful.

I soon get my answer.

A moment later, things grow weird as she starts planting kisses along my neck. Her hand moves down to my belt buckle and she whispers, "I screwed up. Let me make it better, Sammy."

I shudder, my mind going back to the last time I'd been called Sammy, when I was in bed with Jillian. *I will not screw up my chance with her.* I grab Anya's hand and yank it away from my pants.

"Let me make it up to you," she begs.

"No. I came over here to… well, I don't know why I came over here anymore. It definitely wasn't for this." She stands up and tries to remove her top, but I place my hands on her arms, keeping her from removing it completely. "Stop, Anya. Have some respect for yourself. And have some respect for the baby. If you don't want it, give it to someone who will. There are too many women out there aching to be moms."

"Fuck you, Sammy. Get out of here if you don't want

me either. This kid is my ticket to getting Garth to be with me. And if he won't be with me, I'll get a shit-ton in child support from him. Either way, I'll win. And you'll be the lonely loser as always." Her acrid tone reminds me why we aren't together.

"Wow. You know, I thought maybe you had changed. That you might need a friend right now. But you're worse than I ever knew. Have a nice life, Anya."

Before I close the door behind me, she grabs it.

"Don't feel pity for me, Sam. I'm going to come out a winner." She smirks triumphantly.

"I don't feel sorry for you, I feel sorry for your child. They're going to grow up with you as a mother."

She screams obscenities at me as I walk back to my car. As soon as I get behind the wheel, I check my phone. There are no missed calls or texts from Jillian like I'd hoped there would be.

Me: Is it still okay for me to come by tonight?

Jillian: I'm looking forward to it. Bring chocolate chips?

Me: To eat off your body?

Jillian: I was thinking for cookies, but I like your idea.

Me: I'll get enough for both.

Jillian: Sounds perfect. Oh, and you might want to get us more condoms. ;)

Me: On my way to the store now. See you soon.

Why did I ever waste my time going to see Anya? That's an hour of time I could've spent naked with Jillian.

I mentally kick myself for ever thinking it was a good idea.

Seeing Anya pregnant sent me into a tailspin, made me question whether I still care for her. One thing's for sure, the door is closed, padlocked, key tossed, and never to be opened again on whatever I had with Anya. Closure is exactly what I needed.

Jillian is my future, and I'm not looking back.

CHAPTER TEN

JILLIAN

My tunes are playing in the kitchen, currently AC/DC's *Back in Black* album. The kitchen is a mess with the flour, sugar, and all the other ingredients I'd put together before I realized I have no chocolate chips for my chocolate chip cookies.

Waiting on Sam, I left the front door unlocked in case I missed him knocking. Dancing in the kitchen, I don't hear him come up on me. Suddenly, his arms are around my waist and his mouth is on my neck. Placing my hands over his, I move them up to cup my breasts.

He chuckles against my neck. "You don't waste any time, do you?"

When I turned around, my smile fades as I spot lipstick on his collar. I don't want to jump to conclusions like I did with Harrison's butt-dial, so I try to brush away the hurt I'm feeling. "How was your meeting?" I move away from his embrace and turn off the music.

"I'd rather kiss you right now." I place my hand on his chest to stop him and he frowns. "What's wrong?"

"Where have you been today?" I struggle to keep my voice steady. I want to trust him and give him the benefit of the doubt, but I can't stop staring at the pale pink stain mocking me from his neck. The spot *I* want to kiss, yet someone's apparently beat me to it.

Sam sits me down and spills out the events of his day, all the way down to the part where Anya made a move on him.

"How did you ever love someone so horrible?" He doesn't answer, and I know why. We can't control who we fall in love with sometimes.

Sam unbuttons his shirt and says, "I feel funky from today. Do you mind if I take a shower while you finish the cookies?"

"Not at all. I can spray your shirt and put it in the wash."

"Spray it?" He slips it off and examines the material. His eyes widen as he spots the lipstick on the collar. "Damn. Talk about cliché. So that's why you stopped a few minutes ago?"

I cringe. "Sorry. I didn't want to flip out on you automatically, so I waited to see what you said happened today before I jumped to conclusions." Inside, my stomach was doing cartwheels before he told me about his day. I just didn't let it show on my face. No sense in getting mad until there's something to be mad about, right?

"You're amazing, Jillian. You had every right to assume the worst of me. Thank you for giving me the benefit of the doubt." He kisses my hand, and now I know what it means to swoon.

"Amazing" isn't a word I would ever use to describe myself. "Naïve" would probably be an outsider's choice, and might have been mine on a normal day. But I wouldn't dare let this end with Sam over a misunderstanding, which is why I didn't jump to the worst-case scenario as I usually do.

He runs his hands through his hair and lets out a sigh of exasperation. "I can't believe I wanted a kid with her. I mean, it wasn't her at all. Looking back, I know I never loved her. The day she told me she was pregnant though, I saw a future for myself that I'd never imagined before. I wanted—I *still* want to be a dad someday. She stole it from me without even giving me a choice."

The oven timer beeps. Sam looks up at me and over at the oven. "It's preheated."

"You're pouring your heart out to me, Sam. Cookies can wait."

"Cookies should always come first. Go ahead, Jillian."

I dump the chocolate chips in the batter, scoop out a trayful of cookies, place them in the oven, set the timer, and return to the seat next to Sam.

"Did she talk to you before she… did it?" I watch his

eyes fall to the table. I rephrase. "Did she give you a chance to say no?"

"We talked about it, but what was I supposed to say? It's her body. She had the control. I was simply a sperm donor."

As a woman, I understand her side—to a point. When it's your body, you should have the choice on what goes in it or comes out of it. But a woman can't make a baby without a man's involvement in one way or another, and I believe that, in a relationship especially, it should be the choice of both parents. But Sam doesn't need to hear that from me; he only needs me to listen, which is what I will do, even if his shirtless appearance is distracting me slightly. Okay, maybe more than slightly.

"It's been over two years. I thought I was past this. But seeing her knocked up brought the memories crashing back in my mind. Harrison was there for me. He and Carrie took turns letting me cry on their shoulders."

His defense of Carrie makes perfect sense now. They've been around the bend of emotions together, bonding them for life.

"Carrie's a good person." He fidgets with a napkin, twisting it into knots. I know he's thinking about the fight we had a few days ago by how nervous he gets bringing her up.

Resting my hand on his thigh, I soften my voice. "I was hurt by not being invited to the wedding. What I said was wrong of me. She was a good friend to me in college, and I momentarily forgot that."

"She's done a lot for me. And she introduced us, which I

owe her for even more." Cupping my cheek, he smiles. "She doesn't even know yet." Self-conscious as I am, I try not to let it offend me that he hasn't told her about us. Instead, I want to believe he's being a gentleman.

His fingers trace my jawline and his thumb trails over my bottom lip. "We were supposed to be doing something with chocolate chips, not having such a serious conversation."

I let him kiss me briefly before pulling away.

"Tonight, let's talk. After the day you've had, I think you need it more."

A sad smile graces his lips. "You're probably right. Thanks for understanding."

The oven beeps in time for the cookies to still be puffy, barely tanned lumps of dough. Soft cookies are my favorite, so I pull them out to let them finish cooking on top of the stove as they cool. The smell of chocolate fills the kitchen, and I hear Sam take a deep breath before he releases a satisfied sigh. "They smell fantastic."

A few moments later, I carry a plate with four cookies and a glass of milk over to the table. "Let me know if you like them."

Chocolate stains his upper lip as he enjoys the delicious baked treat, and I use the opportunity to take a taste from his lips.

"Bring a plate of those in the living room and let's put in a movie." Sam stands up, grabs the milk from the refrigerator, and pours us each a fresh glass.

"I thought you wanted to talk?"

"I'm through talking about an ex who's not worth my

time and a loss I can't do anything about. I want to be with you, even just sitting on the couch together watching a movie." He mistakes my pause for disapproval, it seems, when he then suggests, "Or we can talk about whatever you want."

"A movie is fine. I was just trying to come up with a good one to watch. Follow me." We walk back to the room of collectibles, and I open the walk-in closet. My movie collection is housed inside, alphabetized by genre. I have a few thousand. "What are you in the mood for?"

"Damn, woman." He peruses the titles and turns to kiss me. "You're seriously the girl of my dreams. Your horror and sci-fi sections are twice the size of your romance one. And the romantic movies you do have are ones I actually enjoy." Seemingly mesmerized by the titles, he fingers each one as he looks for a movie. At the rate we're going, we'll never actually sit down and watch one.

"If you plan to stay all night, we could watch the *Die Hard* series," I offer.

"Minus the fifth one," we state simultaneously. Mouth agape, he shakes his head in surprise. He's learning quickly that I'm not a pink-wearing, fashion-obsessed girly-girl.

Sam sits on the corner of the couch and I grab the opposite corner, leaving a little room between us. After staring at me for a few seconds, he throws his hands in the air. "Fine, if you won't cuddle, I will."

Twisting around, he lays his head on my lap and lets his legs dangle over the other side of the love seat. "You don't mind, do you?" Grinning up at me, he bats his eyelashes flirtatiously.

As the movie starts, he shifts to his side to watch. I run my hands through his hair as the movie progresses. When Alan Rickman comes on screen, we both let out a sad sigh.

We barely get through half of the first movie before the cookies and milk are gone. We elect to skip the second, agreeing part three with Samuel L Jackson is the best.

"My middle name is Linus. I'm not even kidding," he informs me out of the blue.

"Linus? That's so cute. Mine is nonexistent." His head whips around.

"Jillian Nonexistent Hartford? What were your parents thinking?"

I swat his stomach and laugh. "My mom didn't believe in them." He stays facing me now, reaching over to grab the remote and pause the movie. "Bored of watching?"

"No. But I thought we could get to know each other's little things, like what's your favorite color?" His feet swing over the edge of the couch as if he's a kid who can't reach the floor.

"Blue. Specifically cerulean. I think it's mostly because I like saying the name." Sifting my fingers through his hair, I wait for him to answer.

"Mine's green, like the color of your eyes. And that's not a 'get in your pants' line, it's true. Your eyes were the first thing I noticed." Then he grins. "Followed by your ass, of course."

"Of course." His ass was the first thing I noticed, but then again, he *was* flat on his face when we first met. "We already know we like the same movies and music. What about favorite holiday?"

"Christmas" we both agree. "It's only five months away, you know. Do you think we'll spend it together?" Sam's question is so simple but has so much commitment in it.

"I hope so?" I don't question whether I want it, only if it's the answer he wants. The grin on his face has the butterflies fluttering in my stomach.

"Long-term relationships? You know about my one and only."

"Just one for me as well. His name was Jeff. We dated for three years." Talking about him is about the last thing I want to do. Saying things out loud about him always makes me feel like an idiot for staying with him so long.

"Why'd you break up? Not that I'm complaining."

Memories of him jumping up after sex, before I was finished, saying he didn't have all day flit through my mind. The times he said I needed to lose weight because my stomach was too soft. Sam didn't need to hear those things, and I didn't want to repeat them.

"Let's just say my job interfered with his schedule. He wasn't getting enough sex because I was working too many hours." It's what our breakup boiled down to. There just happens to be a longer list, and I gave the CliffsNotes version.

"Tell me about the toughest fire you've gone into."

And things take a turn I hadn't foreseen. No one would accuse me of wearing my heart on my sleeve, and I don't enjoy talking about personal grievances either. My work is private. The only part I've ever shared with Sam was the night he'd been the victim.

Every fire isn't a total loss; occasionally we're called early enough to avoid any damage at all. But sometimes the call you never want to get comes in. The fire you don't want to see, where people are trapped inside and unable to escape. The situations where you think you can save everyone and end up losing it all instead.

I lift his head from my lap and stand up. "Do you want some coffee?" Shuffling into the kitchen, I hear him close behind me.

When I reach for the coffee can, he covers my hand with his. "What did I say?"

"Nothing. Black? Cream and sugar?"

"Jillian, sweetie, your hands are shaking." Taking both of my hands in his, he holds them up to his mouth and kisses my fingertips.

When the tears fill my eyes, he pulls me into his arms and holds me without another word. The question he asked is a memory I wanted to bury.

"Why do you want to hear something so depressing?" No fire is a good one, but the ones where no people are involved are better. Then there are ones none of us want to speak of again. Even around the firehouse we don't reference them. Most of our worst cases involve children.

"I thought since I opened up to you about my past, you might have something you wanted to share." Combing his fingers through my hair, he doesn't press me for the story, for which I'm grateful. I haven't spoken of the memory in four years, and I much prefer it that way.

"Trust me, you don't want the image in your mind. They gave the entire squad mandatory counseling for weeks after. Every day I try to forget it." I grasp the charm on my necklace and close my eyes.

The charm is an angel given to me by my captain, Charles. Being the only female, he thought it would be appropriate. The rest of the men received angel pins for their uniforms. Someone to watch over us. Seeing what we see every day, none of us are particularly religious. But in our field, you're also willing to do anything you can to stay protected. Even if it means putting a little trust in something you aren't sure exists.

"Jillian, I'm really sorry to have brought this all up."

I'm worried that whatever chance I have with Sam may have evaporated with my meltdown.

Swiping my fingers across my eyes, I clear the tears. "You were right. You confided in me about something very painful. It's normal for you to want to hear about my moments too."

And for the next hour, I tell the worst story of my life.

Mid-August, on the first day of school for most of the city, we got the call of a fire at the elementary school two miles from us. We suited up and headed out within minutes.

The school day had ended several hours before, and there was smoke coming from the cafeteria area. One of the lunchroom attendants had left a towel next to a burner that she neglected to notice was still hot.

The fire was localized to the cafeteria, positioned on the bottom level of the school. No one was left in the building because they'd only had a half day. The smoke was noticed by one of the last teachers walking to their car.

Protocol mandated we secure the fire to keep it from spreading. When the building was deemed safe, a team went in to search for any injured parties. We checked the hallway next to the cafeteria first, where smoke had billowed in, but it was empty.

Two classrooms were at the end of the hall, and we needed to get through to see if anyone or anything was missed. As sure as the teachers were that no one was there, we had to be certain. As we worked on the fire, I pushed through to get to the back classrooms. Both doors were locked, and peering through the window, I couldn't see a sign of anyone. We banged on the door, calling out, but heard nothing.

Twenty minutes later, a car pulled up with a frantic mother running toward my chief. "My daughter!" she screamed as she tried to blow past him.

He grabbed her shoulders and said, "Ma'am, calm down. We've been assured the area is clear. Your daughter should be safe. Maybe she rode home with a friend."

"I told her to wait for me in the cafeteria, and my meeting ran long."

My chief ordered us all to look around and help the woman locate her daughter. Soon after, a man pulled up looking for his son. The two were best friends.

"Maybe they're together?" the parents of the two eleven-year-olds tried to reassure each other.

A few moments later, we heard Charles screaming for the paramedics. In his arms was a lifeless boy with soot all over his clothes. Behind him, my friend Barkley had the girl. We'd find out later that they'd been in the back classroom studying while they waited for their rides. When the smoke came into the room, neither of them knew what to do. The boy tried the door but the knob was hot, so they huddled in the far corner of the room. He covered her body with his and tried to shield her from the smoke.

He died saving her life. It was too late for the paramedics, the smoke having damaged his lungs irreparably. The girl had a small burn on her ankle, but the paramedics gave her oxygen to reverse the effects of the smoke. He had blocked her enough to keep the damage to her lungs minimal.

"Eleven years old and he gave his life for someone. You can't imagine the sound of grief that erupted from his father. He sounded like a wild beast. It haunts me to this day."

He lifts my chin with a finger when my eyes drift to the floor. "It's why you came in my apartment after they told you it was empty, isn't it?"

I nod in response. "If I hadn't, I hate to think about what could have happened to you." I close my eyes and take a deep breath. "I'm exhausted. What time is it?"

"Quarter to two. Let's get some sleep. We've both had an exhausting day."

I move toward the bedroom and Sam stays next to the couch.

"Are you coming?"

My invite puts a smile on his face.

"I didn't want to presume."

"I'd never be able to sleep in my bed alone knowing you

were in the other room."

That earns me a soft kiss to my lips, then on my neck, and atop my shoulder. My fingers tracing the line of his chest, and I bite my lip as his hands move to my back. Pulling me close, he rests his head against my shoulder before saying, "Lie down and I'll tuck you in."

I drop my pants and slip under the sheets wearing only panties and my tank top. Sam covers me with a blanket and lies down beside me. I roll over to lay my head against his chest and fall asleep as he combs his fingers through my hair.

CHAPTER ELEVEN

SAM

Lying with Jillian on my chest makes sleeping difficult. Before she slipped her pants off, things were going well. Now all I can think about is her being practically naked against me.

Throughout the night, each time I drift off to sleep, she moves or her leg brushes mine. At one point, she moans my name and presses up next to me, her hand moving down underneath the covers.

"Jillian?" I ask as she rubs me above my boxer briefs. Peering down at her, I see her eyes are still closed. Even so, her hand continues massaging me. "Jillian?" I say louder.

Lifting her head, she groggily asks, "What's wrong?"

Then she looks down at her hand. "Oh. Wow."

"I'm not complaining, but if you want to, I'd rather you be awake."

I roll her onto her back and push myself against her to show the effect her fingers have on me. Dipping my finger down below, I find she's as wet as I am hard. Clearly having thought ahead, she has a condom resting on the nightstand, and I reach over to grab it while she undresses. Once we discard our clothes and find our release together, we're both able to sleep peacefully.

Once I got the call that my apartment could be entered safely, I went to pack what I could. The buildings around mine had structural damage, but mine was still standing with just a lot of smoke damage. There would be a cleaning crew who would have to come in and repair things before anyone could move back in. I packed up my apartment and moved everything to Harrison's for storage until I could find a new place. My lease is almost up, and it's time I found a house instead. My clothes had to go to the dry cleaners to get the smell out of them. Luckily, Harrison and I wear the same size, so he's been sharing his wardrobe with me so I didn't have to buy all new clothes on top of finding a house.

I've been staying at Jillian's for a week now. We always fall asleep together, but I'm usually the first up and out the door. Last night we stayed up rather late working off the grilled cheeseburgers and fries I'd brought home from her favorite restaurant.

At 7:00 a.m., the alarm screams at us to get the hell out of bed already.

"Shit," she exclaims. "I'm due at the station in less than an hour. I guess I hit snooze too many times."

"I never heard it go off," I tell her, which is weird because normally I'm a light sleeper. Most nights I'm an insomniac, unless I'm on sleeping pills or nursing a hangover. None of which happened the night before.

"My alarm reflexes are high. I smack that thing sometimes before it even has a chance to sound. Sorry. I hope I didn't make you late."

On a normal day, I like to be at the office by six thirty so I can beat Harrison there, but I don't mind letting him get the first shot at everything this morning. My view right now is too good to miss. I watch as Jillian slips on her black lace panties and matching bra, enjoying the eyeful of her breasts just before she covers them with the sexy material. She walks to the closet, and as she leans in to grab her clothes, my eyes drift over her firm ass.

"Are you going to watch me dress?" Jillian pauses after pulling on some very stiff dark blue pants.

"Hell yeah. No better view than this, except when the clothes are going in the opposite direction."

Before buttoning her pants, she slips on a button-down shirt of the same stiff material and color. She combs her hair as straight as a stick, slicks it back into a bun, and turns to face me.

"Is that what you wear every day?" My day starts at 4:00 a.m. when I take a run before showering and dressing for work. Being out the door by six, I miss Jillian getting dressed each day. Although, I rather enjoy leaving her naked beneath the sheets, that image lingering in my mind all day.

"It's my uniform, but it's only required certain days of the week. Today I'm wearing it for my hearing."

She quickly shuffles out of the room, and I jump from the bed and run after her.

"What hearing?" I question.

Making as much noise as possible, she fixes a pot of coffee. No one has ever made such noise with a silverware drawer before.

Silence will fall eventually, so I wait it out. When she turns with coffee in hand, I ask again just to be shut out with a loud slurping of the hot drink. "Seriously?"

Heaving a deep, resounding breath, she sets her coffee mug down on the counter. "I have to go before a committee due to my insubordination."

"Insubordination? For what?"

"Disobeying a direct order from my supervisor."

"When did this happen?" I try to think of a conversation where she may have told me this but couldn't remember one.

"Your apartment fire. No one was thought to be in the building. My supervisor ordered me to stay outside because there was no need to risk my safety for an empty structure. He was sure everyone had gotten out, but I wasn't. So I ignored him and went inside. It's a routine disciplinary hearing today for my actions."

And now the concert of the cabinets makes sense.

"For saving me, you mean?"

"It's not about you, Sam. I disobeyed his order for a person. I didn't know you were the person at the time."

No matter how she paints it, I feel at fault.

"Can I speak on your behalf?"

"It's procedural, so there's no need. They have to question me on my reasoning, and when my case is proven, everything will go back to normal." Her lack of eye contact keeps my nerves on high alert.

"And if you don't prove your case?"

"I could lose my title, or possibly my job."

Fuck. All the trouble Jillian is going through is because of me taking stupid sleeping pills. If she loses her job, she'll blame me. She may say she won't now, but I'm not sure she'll feel the same later.

"When you say back to normal… what have you been doing since the fire?"

"Working the phones." I open my mouth, and she places her hand over it. "Sam, don't worry about me. It's how things work. I've been through this before. Whatever the outcome, I'll get through it." She speaks the words so effortlessly, but I see fear in her eyes and feel a tremble in her touch.

"Call me as soon as it's over?"

"I will." Before she walks out the door, she stops at a drawer next to the stove. "Take this and meet me back here tonight. If you want." She tosses a key to me. "It's for the front door. I'll unlock the screen. The alarm code is zero five zero four."

"May the fourth?" We both grin at yet another *Star Wars* reference. "Damn, woman. You're making it hard not to fall in love with you."

The comment is meant to put a smile on her face, not drain the color and cause her to run from the room. But her face pales, her eyes widen, and she's heading for the door, throwing a "See you tonight. I'm gonna be late if I don't go now" over her shoulder.

Not even so much as a kiss goodbye before she slams the door behind her.

"What just happened?" I ask to an empty room. *She* gave me the key. *I* have the penis. *I* should be the one running from commitment, right? Isn't that the way stories usually go? Maybe it's me. Instead of making a woman fall at my feet, I seem to be sending them fleeing out the door.

The *Indiana Jones* theme song plays on my phone. I answer with annoyance in my tone. "Fuck. Harrison, I'm on my way. Jillian… shit." Now the cat's out of the bag.

"Jillian? *She's* the mystery girl? Carrie's college roomie? You've been holding out on us, brother."

"We're not talking about this. I've got to get a shower, and then I'll be in."

I hear the lecture commence as the phone clicks off.

Reading the newspaper when I walk in, Harrison never looks up at me. When I sit in the chair, he drops the paper, folds it neatly, and sets it to the side. Steepling his hands, he uses them to brace himself as he leans over the desk. "You hung up on me, asshole."

"You were *being* an asshole. *Dick.*" Closing my eyes,

I take a deep breath and exhale before saying my piece. "Jillian is amazing. We've been spending time together, and I am infatuated with the woman. She's not only beautiful, but she's also intelligent and funny, and she loves *Star Wars*. She's the whole package, Harrison."

"Are you in love with her?"

"Don't know." I lean back in my chair with my hands behind my head. "One minute I think it's too soon, and then the next I'm picturing her in a white dress." Springing forward, the chair bounces and creaks as I lean in. "I think she'd go for the *Star Wars* theme."

"If she's the one, I'm happy for you, bro." He picks up his phone and punches a few numbers. "And Carrie's going to be happy to know that you two are working out."

Lunging forward, I yank the phone out of his hand. "Nope. No one else knows yet. I don't want everyone putting their two cents in on my relationship. It's me and it's Jillian—period. I'll tell Carrie when I'm ready."

"You want me to lie to my new wife?"

Daphne's voice comes through the intercom. "Your ten o'clock is here, sirs."

We quickly switch to business mode and invite our clients in—a young couple, recently married and looking for a three-bedroom house so they can start a family. During the meeting, as they tell their story, I think about what kind of future home I might want with Jillian. At one point in the meeting, my thoughts come out of my head as I mumble, "Shit." The young man snickers, but the lady looks offended. "I apologize, ma'am. It's just that you made me remember something."

Remember isn't the correct word. More like she's opened my eyes to the realization that I'm falling in love with Jillian Hartford, and there is the distinct possibility that she won't love me back.

CHAPTER
TWELVE

JILLIAN

The hearing goes the way I expect. Questions are posed about my thought process when disobeying my superior officer's orders. After giving my explanation, I assume letting them know the victim remained unharmed would be all I had to prove.

The officiant required witnesses on my behalf. Being friends with most of the guys on the crew, I wasn't worried going in, but the officiant doesn't seem moved by their testimony. The final fact bringing the matter to a close is the sworn testimony of the neighbor I spoke to. My chief obtained a written account from the person and had it signed off.

After the procedural hearing, Captain Marks pulls me aside. "You know I didn't want to bring this matter up, but we had to follow protocol, and too many people witnessed me telling you to remain outside."

"Yes, sir. I understand."

"Hartford, take the rest of the day off. Be at work bright and early in the morning though. Tomorrow we have a couple of kids' parties to do, so wear something fun and appropriate." Before I turn away, he grasps my elbow. "And bring some bubbles. The kids loved them at the last get-together we did."

"I'll see you in the morning."

"Hey, squirt." Jensen Barkley, the junior captain, walks up and pats my shoulder.

"Why do you insist on calling me squirt?" I groan and shuffle my feet childishly, I'll admit it. "You're an entire month older than me and you treat me as if you're twenty years my senior."

"Because it puts a sexy-as-hell scowl on your face. It's fun pissing you off. I can't be the only one who does it. Or am I just the best at it?"

Nope. The award for pissing me off the fastest and the best goes to Sam. Pissing me off is how we ended up in bed together. Come to think of it, our relationship thus far has been built on arguments. Not sure how healthy we really are for one another….

"You okay, Jilli?" Above anyone else in the station, Barkley is my closest friend. He's the big brother I always wanted.

"I'm good. How's the wife?"

Two years ago, Barkley married a girl whom he met at a local trade show. The show is mainly for women, so one of the draws is to have a firemen strip show. It's become increasingly popular over the years. All ages participate, even our sixty-year-old captain.

During the event, we also have a booth set up to collect money for a charity. The year Barkley met his girl, she stuffed a hundred-dollar bill down his pants—all in the name of charity, of course. He French kissed her on stage and waited afterward to get her number.

"Fantastic, as always. There's rumors in the station that you're dating a fire victim. Is it true?"

"Half true. I knew him before the fire."

"Is he the one who caused you to be here today for the hearing?" Concerned for my welfare, I'm sure, he cracks his knuckles as though he's ready to fight someone for me.

"Not his fault. I disobeyed orders. Didn't know it was for him either. Wouldn't change a thing though."

"Hmm. Sounds pretty serious." Barkley follows me out the door and into the parking lot. Stopping just short of my car, he grabs my arm. "Wait a minute, I remember that fire. He's the one who thought we were aliens, isn't he?"

A loud, gruff laugh follows as he looks at me.

Not possessing a poker face is a big flaw of mine.

Sam and I have been seeing each other for over a month now. We haven't officially moved him in, but he's at my place all the time. Most nights I love coming home to find him there, but today has been a rough day. An accident involving five cars happened during rush hour traffic, and my crew rescued a family from a burning vehicle. In the end, everyone was saved, so it was a good day, but there are times that I have trouble putting the work day behind me. The adrenaline, the screams, the smells—they stay with you.

On days like this, I want to curl up in bed and tune the world out. I drive home with the intentions of taking a bath and a nap. The house is empty, which is both disappointing and a relief at the same time. If I came home to find Sam waiting for me, it would've been sweet, but the exhaustion from the day is setting in and I'm a little grouchy. A mental health day is what I need.

I barely have time to relax my muscles before the door opens, Sam bursting through with his hands full of bags. "Honey, I'm home!" he calls out in a terrible accent that I assume is meant to be Cuban, considering the *I Love Lucy* reference.

"Hello, beautiful." My face remains solemn, and he's instantly on alert. "Everything okay?"

"Bad day," I state bluntly.

"Libations to the rescue!" Holding up a six-pack of beer, his smile quickly fades when he sees my expression.

"I don't need someone trying to rescue me, Sam. In case you hadn't noticed, I do a good job of taking care of myself." Days like these, I tend to stay away from people because I start feeling worthless. When I feel down, I push everyone away.

I never rely on anyone but myself. Growing up with a mom who cared more about who her next boyfriend would be instead of taking care of her own daughter, I learned to do everything on my own. When I turned eighteen, I even made my own first gynecologist appointment. The boy I was dating at the time had been pressuring me to have sex, so I needed to make sure I didn't end up pregnant or disease-ridden.

My dad has only ever been good for money. I suppose he thinks if he takes care of me financially, it counts as being a good dad. I see him so infrequently that I didn't know who he was at my college graduation. He introduced himself to me in front of my classmates, who all stared at me with pity in their eyes.

Now Sam wants to take care of me. I have no idea how to let him, so I do what I do best and shut him out instead.

"What happened?" he asks softly, his eyes full of genuine concern.

I prepared myself for an angry response and instead I get kindness. Why doesn't he give up?

I sigh in resignation. "Tough fire. Car accident with a family. I don't want to talk about it."

"Can you let me take care of you for tonight? Let me pamper you? Please?" Happiness sparkles in his eyes and brightens his adorable grin. I wish I could feel his joy right now.

I kick off my shoes and stand in front of him. He's being so sweet, I fight the moodiness and give him a chance to cheer me up.

"What do you have in mind?"

He leads me into the bedroom. "Undress," he commands before walking into the bathroom. For a moment, I feel as though he's not about to pamper me after all, and then I hear the water running. As I take off my clothes, I smell coconut, the scent of my bubble bath—and everything else I use. It's my favorite.

I place a robe around my naked body and head into the bathroom to see what he's up to, finding him lighting candles placed around the room. As he turns to dim the lights, he spots me. "Want me to turn around while you get in?"

"You've seen it all, so what's the point?" I drop the robe and goose bumps pop up everywhere when his half-lidded eyes fill with lust. Gliding my body down into the tub, I sigh as the warm water engulfs me. Bubbles act as a sheet over my body. I scoop up a handful and blow lightly, sending them floating into the air around me.

Sam leaves me there after turning on some music. After a few minutes, I begin to worry he's gone home for the night with how quiet the house is. I close my eyes, and soon I hear "Are you asleep?" whispered softly.

In front of me, he stands holding a cold beer and a bowl of fruit.

"Odd combination, don't you think?" Not a complaint as much as an observation.

"Yeah, but you're not a wine person."

He knows me so well already.

He holds a strawberry up for me, and I wrap my lips

around it, making eye contact with him as I suck on it a moment before biting into it.

"Damn, that was sexy."

He sets the bowl on the corner of the tub and disappears behind me. I take a sip of the beer and sigh as his hands go to work on my shoulders. Surprisingly, the bitterness of the beer mixing with the sweetness of the strawberry creates a great flavor. "You're so tense. Relax," he whispers against my ear.

"You could join me in here."

You can imagine my disappointment when he responds, "It's all about you tonight. I'm spoiling you."

"What if I want to be pampered by you with no clothes on and covered with bubbles?" Leaning my head back against the tub, I peer up at him. He leans down to give me a kiss. Sucking on my bottom lip first, he then tries to slip his tongue inside but hits teeth. We both start laughing. "Mary Jane and Spiderman made the upside-down kiss look much sexier."

Sam stands, slips off his shirt, and shimmies out of his pants. "We'll just have to make bubble baths sexier."

I gulp down a swig of beer and lick my lips.

"Full Sammy, my favorite." I grin as he lowers himself into the tub. My mood is already lightening.

With my last relationship, spontaneity wasn't a thing. Because of my hectic schedule, he expected sex on the nights I was off, and like the well-behaved girlfriend, I obliged. Looking back, I think about how toxic the whole thing was. When I had moods like today, he wouldn't try to cheer me up; instead, he'd tell me I was being a bitch and would go off on his own for the night.

With Sam, I never feel the obligation to do anything. He doesn't expect more than I can or want to give. It's easy with him. It's real. And we may not have been together long, but as he dips into this water with me, his leg sliding against mine, I feel the electric spark rush through my entire body.

Together, naked, wet, and he still hasn't made a move other than to relax me.

He shifts around with his back to me. "Do you want to get behind me?" I ask.

"Nope." When he slides back against my chest, I suck in a breath when his skin makes contact with my nipples. Draping my arms over his shoulders, he sighs. "Let's stay this way."

"First we'll grow pruny. Then the water will get cold, and eventually we'll be hungry." I pepper kisses against his hair after every few words.

"If I died pruny, frozen, and starved, at least I'd have died happy." Sweet words from anyone else would send me into doubt, but hearing them from Sam makes me want to tell him how I feel.

Pondering my thoughts, I open my mouth to take a chance on love, as Adam would say. "I think—"

And his phone rings.

"Hold that thought, gorgeous." He leans forward and grabs the phone, eyes widening a bit when he sees the caller ID. The first thing he says is "Anya? What happened?"

Lifting himself from the tub, his naked form is something

to behold as bubbles glide down his muscles. He wraps a towel around his waist and leaves the room as though I'm no longer there.

So much for a relaxing evening.

The mood has been ruined, so I towel off and grab my robe from the hook. Gazing in the mirror as I comb through my wet locks, I note the despair in my eyes. A glimpse of the future I have with Sam. A nonexistent one if his ex gets her way. And since I stand alone in my room while she occupies his attention, it seems she's won this round.

The towel Sam had been wearing hangs on the chair and his clothes are gone. I tiptoe lightly through the house, listening for him. He left me naked and wet, so I feel justified in my eavesdropping.

"No. I've told you she means nothing to me." A pause and then he replies, "It was sex, and not even great sex. I thought it could be something, but I was wrong." A dramatic sigh and he says, "Yes, I'll do my best to let her down gently. I have to go."

Not wanting him to know I overheard him, I step back into my second bedroom and hide against the wall until he passes.

"Jillian?" he calls out. Quickly, I sprint across the hall to the bathroom and enter through the door in the hall before he comes through the one in my bedroom. He frowns. "You're dressed."

"Pruny," I state, holding up my hand for proof. All I want is to be alone. If what I overheard means he's going to reject me, I don't want it to happen tonight. "I'm tired and would like to go to bed. Do you mind?" I may have given him a chance to explain if my mood wasn't already crappy, but I just can't deal with this right now.

"Not at all," Sam says, moving toward me. Just as he reaches for my waist, I step back. "What's wrong?" His eyebrows furrow with concern.

"I'd like to be alone tonight. I hope you don't mind." I walk down the hall and open the door before I notice he isn't following me. "Sam?" I call out.

Peering around the corner, he looks shell-shocked. "What's happening?"

"I'm asking you to leave. How hard can that be to comprehend?" Anger is the best defense mechanism I can use to keep from breaking down. But treating him badly feels like I swallowed a boulder. My stomach aches and I want to apologize, but I don't have the energy.

"We were having a good time a few minutes ago...." Sam leaves it hanging, almost as if it's a question.

Opening the door, I prop my hip against it, waiting for him to pass. "Thanks for the massage. It was... nice." I know what I heard on the phone, but looking at his face right now—the confusion, the hesitation, but most of all the pain in his eyes—gives me pause. "I'm sorry. It's been a long day, and I don't want to take it out on you."

He stands tall, clears his throat, and walks out of my house. "I'll call you later, then. Get some sleep. Maybe I could bring breakfast by?"

"I think I just want a few days to myself. I need to unwind." Sam nods slightly and leans in for a kiss, but I turn my face so his lips land on my cheek. "Good night."

The moment the door closes, the sobs release. My palm closes over my mouth, trying to muffle the sound. I want to believe I misunderstood what I heard, but the ache in my heart is telling me I let my walls down too quickly with him.

CHAPTER
THIRTEEN

Harrison and Carrie didn't expect me home this evening, so of course I walk in to find them having sex on the kitchen counter. Luckily, they don't see me—though I can't unsee them—and I'm able to tiptoe back to the guest room for the night.

"At least someone's getting laid tonight," I mutter. Of course, I hadn't planned on having sex with Jillian, but I did expect to be sleeping with her. Her day had been sucky, and I wanted to be her knight in shining armor to make it better. I hope her dismissal of me can be chalked up to a bad mood.

I start to text her and stop myself. She wants time alone, and I will respect her wishes. Her mood swing has me flummoxed though. Our night was going so well for a while. Maybe when I left her alone, it gave her time to think about her day and put her back in a foul mood.

Tomorrow I plan to show up at her house for breakfast whether she likes it or not. I know people have given up on her in the past, and I'm not going to repeat history for her.

The moans from the other room grow louder. They must have moved to the couch. I put in my headphones and drift off to the not-so-mellow tunes of Metallica. Hopefully they figure out I'm in here before they try to christen my room along with the rest of the apartment. As soon as the insurance company completes my claim for my loss of living space, I'll be able to go full force looking for a new place. Truthfully, I could've gotten my own place by now, but I'm trying to see how things go with Jillian first. If she's ready to settle down, we could find a house together.

Things with Jillian have moved fast in comparison to my other relationships, but she's perfect for me. I've never felt more comfortable with someone, never been able to laugh so freely, and we're practically the same person with the amount we have in common. Being with her is the only time I can just be myself.

And in that moment, I sit up and stare straight ahead at the wall. "Holy shit, I'm not *falling* in love with Jillian Hartford. I'm already there." And tomorrow when I see her, I'll tell her. It'll either brighten her mood or she'll let me down—hopefully more gently than the way she sent me off tonight.

It's Carrie who figures out I spent the night when I walk into the kitchen around two in the morning to find her stark-naked eating a chicken leg. Her scream wakes Harrison, who races into the kitchen and swings his fist toward my face. My reflexes are better than his aim, thankfully, so I'm able to duck before he makes contact.

"What the hell, Sam?" Carrie slaps my arm with one hand while the other holds an apron to cover her body. "You scared the crap out of me. Try calling when you're coming home."

"If you two hadn't been christening the kitchen when I got home tonight, you'd have known I was here."

"I thought you'd be at Jilli's. Is everything good with you two?" *Now* she shows concern, when a moment ago she was ready to pummel me. I glare at Harrison but decide not to scold him for sharing my secret when I asked him not to.

"She had a bad day and wanted time alone."

"Come sit. Let's talk." Clearing his throat, Harrison points at Carrie's attire. Flittering her hands around, she says, "Well, he's seen it all now. What's a few more minutes?"

"Go put clothes on. I don't want him ogling you."

She sighs and struts away shaking her naked ass in Harrison's direction.

Carrie's a beautiful woman, and I might have stared harder at her body if she didn't feel like a sister. Plus, Jillian is the only one I want to see naked these days. The woman has me totally whipped, and in such a short amount of time. I wonder if Harrison felt the same way when he realized

Carrie was "the one."

"Is this better, sir?" Carrie snarks when she returns in a T-shirt of Harrison's that reaches her knees.

"Pants would be better, but—" He nips at her neck, grazing it with his teeth. "—I like when you call me sir." Giggles from Carrie mingle with growls from Harrison.

"I'm still here! Damn, you two are like animals." Carrie grabs my hand as I start to leave the room. "We can talk another time," I say, trying to give her an out.

"No, we can't. Sit. I turned on the coffee pot when I got up earlier so I could make a cup of cocoa."

The blue light of the coffee machine flashes, letting me know the water is heated. "Hot cocoa, bro?"

"Only if you put whiskey in it," Harrison responds.

"Is there any other way to drink it?" We each fill a glass mug with cocoa and a shot of whiskey, then take a seat at the table with Carrie.

"What happened to make Jillian push you away?" Blowing lightly on her drink, Carrie peers up at me above her mug. "I lived with her for three years, Sam. She spooks easily. And if she feels things aren't going her way, she'll bow out first as a protection for herself. If she thinks you're going to leave, she'll leave you first."

"She had a rough day, that's all. When she came home, I kind of threw myself into pampering her, and I think I overwhelmed her." I relay the night's events to Carrie. Well, not all of them. Some of the intimate details should stay between me and Jillian.

"Sounds pretty harmless. Maybe she did just need space."

Shrugging, she leans back and sips on her nonalcoholic cocoa.

"Did you figure out what you're going to do about Anya?" Harrison chimes in. He's more preoccupied with getting Anya out of my life than I am. As far as I'm concerned, we were over a long time ago.

"Wait, what happened with Anya?" Carrie asks.

So apparently my brother hasn't told her *all* my business yet.

"She stopped by the office looking for him. Acted all high and mighty, telling me how mad Sam would be with how I treated her because they're getting back together." Harrison conveniently left out the crappy things she voiced about Carrie and trying to convince my brother of the possibility that the child is mine. Not sure how she thought he would believe it, but she's desperate for attention.

"Over my dead body would he go back to that trash," my sweet Southern belle sister-in-law spouts. She's very protective of me when it comes to Anya.

"Over mine too, Leia." I turn to Harrison and say, "Like I told you on the phone, she and I had a purely sexual relationship. I understand that now. She meant nothing to me. I'm going to let her down easy."

My brother seems content with my reiteration, but Carrie's eyelids lower into slits.

"When did you talk to him on the phone?" she asks.

"Earlier at the office," Harrison replies.

"I mean where were you, *Sam*?" Carrie asks.

"At Jillian's. I got the call while we were in the tub,

then left the room to talk about it." Her head bobs in understanding, though she still appears deep in thought. "Why?"

"When did Jillian become cold and aloof?" she asks.

"I don't know," I bite back, as her questions are beginning to annoy me. "A few minutes later."

"Did she ask who was on the phone? Or did you tell her it was Harrison?"

"Carrie, what the hell is with the twenty questions? Do you need me to spell it out second by second?" Frustrated, I stand up ready to escape to my room.

She grabs my hand. "Humor me, please."

"I answered the phone. Before I could say hello, Harrison said, 'Your pregnant ex-girlfriend paid me a visit just now,' and I asked, 'Anya?'"

Her nails dig into my skin suddenly. "Wait. So for your end of the conversation, the first thing you said was Anya's name with a confused tone. And then you left the room?"

This storytelling thing is getting old fast.

"Sam. You're not this dense. She thought you were talking to Anya. And she probably heard you say the part about it just being sex, and she thinks it's about her."

"That's ridiculous. She should know I feel more for her than just a booty call."

"Have you told her? Contrary to what we say, we don't always know everything," she points out.

Come to think of it, we haven't had a talk about where we stand. Maybe she *did* think I meant it about her.

I rise from the chair with determination. "I have to call

her and tell her how I feel."

"Whoa, Cassanova. It's three in the morning. It can wait until a more reasonable time," Carrie assures me. "Go do it face-to-face and make it special."

I take my sister-in-law's advice and decide to go to bed. And I stare at the ceiling for at least three hours, watching the clock tick over to six before I fall asleep.

Due to my long hours of ceiling gazing, I sleep well past noon.

So much for taking breakfast over and confessing my love over a donut. Due to the late hour, I decide a text is important to get the ball rolling on things getting back to normal.

Me: Good morning, beautiful

I wait for a response, but it doesn't come immediately. I get in the shower to keep my mind off things as I wait for her reply. When I step out, I check my phone and see a new message.

Jillian: It's afternoon.

Ouch. It's apparent by the short, humorless answer that she's still upset with me.

Me: I missed sleeping next to you last night.

I see the text bubbles appear, disappear, and reappear again. And then nothing.

Me: I want to see you tonight, if you feel up to it. We could watch a movie and order in.

Jillian: I could be up for that.

Her replies are different than they've been lately. I realize she's putting up her walls again. Like Carrie said, she's pushing me away by acting nonchalant about everything. It'll take more than words to prove to her how I feel. If I run over there bringing up the phone call, it'll sound as though I'm making excuses or planned a story overnight to cover myself. I'll have to show her she's the one I want to be with and Anya is my past. If I give her too long to think, she'll find an excuse to get out of tonight.

Romance is the mood I'm going for, so I put on my best navy pinstripe suit and grab a single red rose on my way over to her house. It looks like the neighbor's having a party next door; the driveway is full and spilling over into Jillian's yard.

I knock on her door, trying to peek through the peephole, then the windows. No sign of her. I place the rose through the door handle, take out a business card, and write "I hope you're having a better day today, beautiful." I slip the card behind the rose and walk back toward my car.

The party next door is rather distracting with all the laughter and playful screaming, and I begin to wonder if she couldn't hear me knock due to the noise. I start around to the back door just as Jillian steps out the front. I see her from the corner of my eye and turn back around.

She lifts the rose and looks at my car. The card's on the ground, so she misses it entirely. Her eyes drift over me and then stop when she realizes I'm standing there. Her mood deflates when she sees me, her body slumping as she tries to avoid looking at me. I miss her beautiful smile. The only word I can find is "Hi."

"Um, hi." I'm speechless. She's standing on her front porch wearing a triangle bikini top and short, yet not too revealing bottoms. She has a towel thrown over her shoulder.

"Where are you going dressed like that?" Even I notice the jealousy searing in my voice.

She takes a deep breath and, instead of biting my head off for being a tool—which would be highly justifiable, based on my tone—she smiles. "Next door for a swim. What are you doing here?" The smile is forced; it doesn't meet her eyes. She's holding back to keep me from seeing her pain. I know her true smile too well.

"I wanted to spend the day with you." Motioning to her outfit, I say, "I feel a bit overdressed right now."

"Is this from you?" She holds up the rose.

"Yes. I feel like I haven't wooed you enough." I wink. I see a hint of a true smile beginning to form.

"Do you have to work today?" I shake my head. "Come over and swim."

"And meet the infamous Stephan finally?" I tease. As much time as I've spent at her house lately, we haven't run into him. Or maybe it's that she doesn't want us to meet for some reason.

"Stephan is out of town. I invited some friends over." I gesture to the suit jacket and furrow my brow. "You could always skinny-dip," she suggests coyly.

"Um...."

"Relax, I'm only half serious." She winks. "Stephan probably has something you can borrow. If you want to meet my friends." She bites her lip, a habit she does when she's nervous or horny; currently it's the nervous one. I can tell because her eyes dip to the ground. When she's horny, the bite is coupled with a rosy blush across her chest and a sly smile.

I'm as nervous about meeting her friends as she is for me to meet them. She's told me before her friends are all firefighters and they're her family as well. Meeting them is the equivalent of meeting the parents. It's my chance to prove to her I'm in this for real.

I step closer to her, wishing to hell that all the friends next door were women, because I can't stand the thought of any other guy seeing her wearing so little.

"We could go inside first, have a few moments alone." I lean down to kiss her bare shoulder, and she tenses. Maybe she still thinks I'm only after sex with her. I need to make sure she knows it's not the case. "I wanted to talk to you about something."

"Can it wait? I'm running late already. Stephan entrusted his house to me. I should be over there. Do you want to come or not?" She sounds so unsure of herself. I can't believe things took such a turn with a simple misunderstanding.

"I'd love to. Let's see if I can wear his suit."

Following her next door, she leads me into the bedroom and shows me the closet. I'm a little weirded out by how well she gets around his room for someone she's never been attracted to, but I'm taking the leap to trust her. She's given me no reason not to.

"Come outside when you're dressed, and I'll introduce

you to everyone."

Five minutes later, I'm staring at myself in the mirror wearing swim trunks that are a little snug, with a Hawaiian flower pattern design. They have a price tag on them, so I rip it off and decide I'll replace them for him. Wearing used swim trunks would be like borrowing underwear—way too creepy.

I walk through the living room to the back door, and my mouth drops open at the scene in front of me. There are at least fifteen shirtless, muscular guys acting crazy and splashing around. Jillian waves me outside, and I quickly snap out of it. Hopefully I didn't embarrass her with my window-peeping moment.

"This is a total sausage fest," I mumble to her.

"There are a few tacos too," she says, pointing to two women sitting on the edge of the pool being attended to by who I'm assuming are their significant others.

"Hey, Sam!" A face I recognize, Adam from the hospital, strolls up with another man in tow. "This is my husband, EJ."

I pump his hand, and he nudges Jillian's arm. "You're right, he's a keeper." A rosy hue fills her cheeks as she smiles at him.

"How long have you two been married?" I ask.

Adam grasps EJ's hand. "Almost a year."

"I've heard many great things about both of you from my husband. I was happy to get the chance to meet Jilli today."

Jillian grins at the two men, then looks to me once more.

"It's easy to see why they fell in love. They're both so great. I told them we'd like to…." Her gaze falls to the side, away from me.

A crease forming in his forehead, Adam stares at Jillian and finishes her sentence for her. "We'd like to double-date sometime. Right, Jilli?"

Sliding my hand into hers, I smile at her before saying, "A double date sounds great." And then I change the subject. "How is Mikayla doing?" Ever since the day at the hospital, the little girl has been on my mind.

"The moment her mom woke up, Mikayla told her all about Percy the Penguin and the cool guy Sam who brought him to her. She has such a crush on you." He elbows Jillian's side. "You have competition."

Just as she's about to speak, one of the overly buff men springs forth from the pool as though he can fly, lifts Jillian from behind, and throws her in the deep end.

"Looks like I have competition too." I hadn't necessarily meant to say it out loud, but nevertheless, it's out there now.

"That's Tucker," Adam replies as Jillian's head pops back up. "They're practically siblings." Jillian flings her hair back, and I watch Tucker lick his lips and sneak a peek at her cleavage. "Um, well, she thinks of him as a brother, at least. She's told me as much."

Even though Tucker can't seem to take his eyes off my girl, her eyes meet mine. "Come on in and cool off."

Tucker grabs her from behind, draping his arms around her neck. His hands are too close to her breasts for my comfort. She's laughing and trying to reach behind her to dunk him, but he keeps his hold on her. My jaw tightens as his arm dips below the water and Jillian lets out a playful scream, dunking down in the water and breaking free of him.

Adam leans forward and whispers, "She's crazy about you, Sam. No one else."

I take two steps back. Sprinting forward, I jump off the edge, pulling my legs up beneath me and landing butt first in the pool, sending a giant splash right over Tucker's face. Petty, but fun.

When I come up for air, Jillian moves closer to me and drapes her arms over my neck. "You going to introduce me to anyone else today?" I ask. "Perhaps your recent attacker?"

She tosses her head back in laughter and yells out, "Everyone, this is Sam. Sam, everyone." Leaning in toward my face, she adds, "Tucker is the guy you drenched to defend my honor. He's harmless. And nothing to be jealous about."

"I'm not jealous, just protective." I press my lips against her ear so no one else can hear me. "Do these guys know I'm the one who they saved on sleeping pills?"

One of the bald, muscular, ebony gods to my right shouts, "Look out, Sam, alien invasion!" and jumps in the pool.

Jillian sucks her lips between her teeth, trying not to smile. "No," she lies. "Not a single one remembers." With a quick kiss, she pulls away, but I whisk her back against the current of the water and enjoy a much longer kiss. Catcalls and whistles erupt around us. Surprisingly, the loudest comes from Tucker. I suppose he *is* nothing to worry about.

The guy who just jumped into the pool swims up to me. "Hey, Sam, do you know anything about grilling? Jake here usually does it for us, but he burns everything." He reaches out for me. "I'm Barkley."

We shake, and I climb out of the pool to help. I notice Jillian gives him a wink, and I wonder if I'm about to experience hazing. While I'm working the grill, I see Jillian slip inside, returning a few minutes later with a tray full of fruit and veggies before heading back into the kitchen.

"Can you watch the grill for me, Barkley?" Handing him the spatula, I go inside to grab a plate to put all the meat on. Plus, it will give me a moment by myself with Jillian.

I stop when I hear voices in the kitchen, and I peer around the corner to see what's going on.

Tucker has Jillian cornered at the counter. She's being polite and smiling, but I can see she's uncomfortable. She isn't the only one; his close proximity to her is making my blood boil.

Cape at the ready, I'm about to swoop in to her rescue when I see her place a firm hand on his chest. "I've tried to be nice, Tucker. I'm not interested. I'm sort of seeing someone, and you need to back off."

Sort of seeing?

"He's not one of us, Jill." He takes her hand off his chest, and I see it disappear just as he leans in to kiss her. I take two steps forward, and he cries out in pain. Bent over with his face close to her chest, he's begging her to stop.

Now I see her hand is on his crotch and she's squeezing so hard her knuckles are white. I cover my mouth to keep from laughing and cringe at the thought of his pain. "You touch me again, or try to make me do something I don't want to do, and I will report you to the captain so fast your head will spin."

"Not to mention her boyfriend will kick your ass too."

Jillian lets go and stares up at me entering the kitchen. Tucker's hand covers his junk as he falls into a chair nearby.

Placing my finger in his face, I say, "She can obviously take care of herself just fine. But if you ever touch her again without her permission, I will throw down a little pain of my own just for fun."

Tears fill his eyes. He nods and rises from the chair, then hobbles outside.

"Are you okay?" I step a little closer, but leave her some personal space after the incident just now.

"Like you said, I can take care of myself."

I admire her spunk. "You don't play around. You went straight for the nuts."

"Well, he has no one to blame but himself. He placed my hand on his dick as though I'd been waiting for it."

My face flames with angry heat. Whether she can take care of herself or not is beside the point.

I turn to march outside to teach Tucker a lesson, but Jillian grabs my arm. "Please stay with me. Earlier you said you wanted to talk. What was that about?"

I know she's just trying to distract me, but we have a minute alone so I'm taking advantage of it. "I want to know what happened last night. What made you push me away and build those walls again?"

She drops her hold on my arm. "Who called you last night?"

"Harrison. Anya stopped by his office spouting a bunch of lies about us getting back together. He was freaking out a bit about it. I had to reassure him there was never love there. I'm supposed to call her, but I don't want to speak to her again." My finger grazes her shoulder. "I was up most of the night talking with Carrie. She gave me some good advice."

"What kind of advice?"

"Mostly about patience. Last night freaked me out, Jillian. I wasn't sure if I did something wrong. I just knew I wanted to fix whatever was broken."

Her eyes dip to the ground, and she says, "Sometimes I think *I'm* broken. I jump to crazy conclusions, like I did when you were on the phone. I've always had issues handling things well. Even what happened with Tucker earlier."

"He had no right to touch you that way, regardless of whether you have a boyfriend or not." My nostrils flare, and I feel my blood pressure rising all over again.

Jillian places her hands against my cheeks, cupping them gently. Just the feel of her skin against mine calms me.

Her lips curl into a smirk. "There's that word again. Boyfriend. Who is my boyfriend?"

"Maybe this will jog your memory."

Our lips meet, and I back her into the counter until she has to hop up on it. Sliding between her legs, I glide my hands along her skin, moving across her stomach until I push her top above her breast and capture her nipple with my mouth.

"Sam," she gasps. "Everyone's outside."

I move my free hand between her thighs and slide it under the fabric. She opens her legs and bucks against my hand when I slip my finger inside her.

"Still want me to stop?" I bite down on her nipple, causing a moan of pleasure to escape. Her hand dips into my swim trunks, and she pumps my erect cock. "I'll take that as a no."

We work at one another with the backdrop of the party outside. The danger of being caught makes it hotter. "I want you, Jillian."

"Take me." She lowers herself from the counter and kneels on the floor. She takes me in her mouth, and I'm ready to explode the moment her tongue swirls the head. I force myself to hold back so I can be inside her.

"I'm not going to last if you keep doing that. We need a condom."

An audible pop sounds as she stops sucking. "I'm on the pill and I'm clean. Do we still need one?"

I shake my head.

She stands, turns around, and bends forward over the table. Moving her bikini bottoms to the side, I press into her from behind. My hands cup her breasts, hers gripping the table's edge, the table rocking back and forth with my thrusts. Reaching her peak, she cries out, and I quickly place my hand over her mouth to muffle the sound. As I empty inside her, I release a low growl of satisfaction. I help her up off the table. She grabs a hand towel from a nearby drawer and some cleaner and freshens up the table we just christened. I chuckle, knowing I've never met Stephan though I've been very intimate with his furniture.

We straighten our suits—I'm definitely keeping this one now—and I grip her hand in mine. "Let's head back outside."

Jillian pulls back on me. "So, we're calling this a relationship, then? A boyfriend-girlfriend thing?"

"Yes, if you want it as much as I do, and believe me, I want you to be mine. *Only* mine." Dragging my finger across her cheek, I watch as her eyes light up when the smile reaches them. The metaphorical walls come down once more. And we're back on track as though the events of last night never happened.

CHAPTER
FOURTEEN

It doesn't appear as though anyone at the party even noticed we were gone. They're all munching on burgers when Sam and I head back outside. Barkley tells me that Tucker left, saying he didn't feel well.

The sun begins to set soon after we rejoin the group, and one by one, the rest of the crew leaves. Adam and EJ are the last to take off, making us promise we'll double-date sometime. Earlier I stopped myself from mentioning it to Sam because I still wasn't sure where we stood. Now the talk is out of the way, the "boyfriend" word has been used, and things are back to great between us.

I plop myself down in a chair with one leg bent and the

other straight out, closing my eyes for a moment. Feeling something touch my foot, my eyes spring open. Sam smiles and pulls my foot into his lap, giving it a massage.

"You know what's great for sore muscles?" He doesn't wait for me to guess. "Water. Let's take a dip before we leave." He stands and removes his trunks before jumping in stark-naked.

I slip my bikini off and follow him in. Now I can mark skinny-dipping off my bucket list.

Pushing my way back to the surface, I gasp for air, my teeth chattering with the chill of the water. Without the sun, the temperature of the water has gone down. Sam moves closer and envelops me in his arms from behind. We float around the pool together, enjoying the closeness of our bodies, the cool caress of the water, and the beautiful moon showing its face tonight.

"Jillian, I—"

"Ahem. Looks like I missed a great party." Stephan's presence startles me, and I jump from Sam's arms. "And skinny-dipping."

Wrapping my arms around my naked chest, I look at Sam, who's chuckling. Glad he finds this humorous.

"We were about to clean up. Stephan, this is Sam." They shake hands just before Stephan hands him the trunks to put on. He drops my bikini next to the pool and turns to let us dress. "You're home early. Did everything go okay?"

"Yeah, just finished business early. I wanted to come home and hang out with you and the guys. I'm sorry I missed them. Do you two want to stick around for a bit?"

He holds up a six-pack. "I brought beer."

"I'm in. Sam?"

He nods, so we dry off, then clean the outside area, disposing of all the trash and evidence of the party earlier. Stepping inside the kitchen door, I inhale and sigh. "You brought pizza too. I hope it's enough to share, I'm famished."

"I bet you are." Stephan winks. "Come help me in the kitchen." I follow him while Sam makes himself comfortable on the couch. "I see things are going quite well with the sexy realtor?" he says when we're out of earshot.

"We're exclusive, so yeah, I'd say so."

"Exclusive? What language are you speaking?" Stephan winks and nudges my ribs.

The guys hit it off immediately. They're both hockey fans, something I didn't know about either. Their favorite team is the Nashville Predators, the local home team. Apparently they've made it into the Stanley Cup playoffs. By the time they finish talking about hockey, I'm three beers in. The topic changes to football, and I lay my head back against the couch and prop my feet on Sam's lap. Without stopping the conversation, he rubs my feet. I catch an impressed look from Stephan.

Sports have never been my thing. I've given a few of them a chance, but haven't found one to hold my interest. Now if someone starts a real-life quidditch league, sign me up.

Then they begin discussing my collectible toys. I want to chime in, but I'm too exhausted from being in the water all day and from the beer. When I yawn several times in the span of a few minutes, Sam places his arm around my back and the other under my knees, lifting me into his arms. I wrap my hands around his neck and rest my head on his shoulder. "You're so strong."

He chuckles and kisses my forehead.

"Good night, Stephan. It was great meeting you. Dinner tomorrow night?"

"I'll be there, man," he answers.

I barely remember anything else. Even the walk to my house is a blur.

The next morning, I awake in an empty bed. On the nightstand is the red rose I found on my doorstep the day before, with a note.

Good morning, beautiful. I hated to leave you without saying goodbye, but you looked so peaceful as you slept. I'll be by for dinner tonight after work. Stephan's coming over. I hope you have an amazing day. – Yours, Sam.

Unfortunately, I didn't get to tell him I'm working second shift today. I send him a quick text.

Me: I'll be at work until 8 tonight. Hang out with Stephan until I get home if you want. I can pick up takeout on the way. Chinese ok?

Sam: Sounds great. Are you hungover this morning?

Me: No. Sad I missed seeing you though.

His next text is a picture of him with his hair messy and a grin on his face.

Sam: Here's a pic of me with bedhead. Feel better?

Me: It definitely perks me up. See you tonight.

I want to type those three little words I've been trying to say to him, but texting it the first time seems tacky. Plus, I need to see his face to be sure he feels the same.

CHAPTER
FIFTEEN

Last night I carried Jillian home, tucked her into bed, and lay beside her watching her sleep. This morning, I'm paying the price by being exhausted. I'm currently on my second cup of coffee, with a shot of espresso, when I get her text. No longer do I need coffee to perk me up.

Since she won't be home until late, it will give me time to talk to Stephan a little more. I want to run an idea by him and see if he thinks she'll love it or hate it. At first mention of him, I admit I had been a bit green-eyed, but after getting to know him a little better, I have no doubt he's just a good friend and nothing more.

My work day is rather boring. No clients come in, so I

spend the day catching up on paperwork and sending faxes, then update the website with the listings we received this week. By noon, I'm ready for any sort of human interaction. Daphne has the day off, and Harrison took the afternoon to be with Carrie, so when two o'clock rolls around without a single phone call, I lock up and head to Jillian's. I know she isn't home, but I can take a nice nap before she gets off and still catch Stephan with plenty of time.

Her house is quiet, though I'm not sure what I expected. In a way, it feels more like home to me than anywhere I've lived recently. I kick off my shoes, hang my suit jacket by the door, and remove my tie, sinking down into her plush couch. Still pumped full of caffeine, I channel-surf for a bit before eventually landing on a talk show. Turning to the side, I prop my feet on one end of the couch and lay my head down on the other.

Sometime during the talk show, I fell asleep. Woken up by my own snores, I sit up to stretch and crack my neck and back. It's after five now and the news is on. Standing slowly, I head to the kitchen to grab a drink when someone starts banging on the door. The knocks sound frantic, so I set the glass down and rush over to see who it is.

"Hey, man, I was just coming over to see you," I say to Stephan, who ignores me and bursts into the room, looking around. "What's up?"

"Is Jillian here?"

"No, she's at work. I wanted to talk to you about something. Are you okay?"

His eyes are all over the place, and his hands are fidgeting frantically. I wonder if he's on something.

"I was hoping you wouldn't say that." Taking his phone out, he dials a number and curses. "She's not answering her phone. When was the last time you talked to her?"

"You're freaking me out."

The news reporter grabs my attention when she breaks in with a story. "We're following this breaking story closely to give you the most current information. Firefighters are still working to put out what they assume is an electrical fire. The office building under construction in downtown Nashville erupted in flames this morning. As the fire increased, part of the building collapsed with two firefighters trapped inside. We have no names to release at this time due to the families needing to be notified first."

I immediately do the same thing Stephan's been doing and dial Jillian. No answer, straight to voice mail. It means nothing. She turns her phone off for work all the time, and most likely it's in her locker or the truck. Everyone she knows is probably calling her right now.

The news reporter continues. "This just in, the two firefighters are not responding to their radios or any of the voices calling for them. A team is being assembled to go in for them after the area is secured. At this point, we don't know if it will be for rescue or recovery." Her tone drops to one of sadness, as if she might know either of the victims personally.

"I'm going down there." I grab my keys and head for the door, but Stephan grasps my arm.

"Wait. I'm coming with you."

Glad to have someone to help me bear this possible

burden, I welcome his company. On the way, I have him text Harrison and Carrie, who offer to meet me at the site. He tells them I'll keep them updated but to stay away for now, that the less people who show up, the better.

Stephan offers to drive, but he's shakier than I am, though I'm not sure how. I think it's too unreal for me now, and I'm hoping for the best.

As we get off the interstate, I can see the billows of black smoke filling the sky. Still blocks away from the fire, the traffic is at a standstill with everyone trying to be nosey or, like us, trying to find out about a loved one.

"Who is Jillian's emergency contact?" I ask, hoping Stephan knows how to reach them.

"I don't know. Her mom lives up north, and her dad only gives her money and nothing else." I feel bad not knowing these things about her life. "I would think, if it's anyone, it's me. I use her as mine anytime I need one. It's possible it's you. You two have spent a lot of time together lately."

Focusing on the idea of being her emergency contact, I convince myself that she's not one of the trapped people or else they would call me. As if on cue, my phone rings and I jerk in surprise, causing the car to swerve.

"Relax, it's just Harrison calling." My heart starts back up as Stephan answers the call. "Nothing yet, man. We're trying to get through traffic. Still six blocks away. I'll tell him." Stephan hangs up and says, "Carrie is trying to track down people who know Jillian too, just in case she can find out something."

I pull up next to a driveway for a liquor store. Stephan

eyes me and says, "Drinking may not be the best idea right now."

"I'm turning the car over to you. Get there when you can. I'm running the rest of the way. I need to know she's safe. I'll call you as soon as I find out something."

He nods and climbs out of the car as I jump out of my seat and open the rear door.

I unbutton my dress shirt, leaving just an undershirt on, and toss it in the back seat before sliding in to remove my pants and slip on shorts from my gym bag. Trading out my dress shoes for tennis shoes, I say a quick goodbye to Stephan, and I'm off.

Jillian's face flashes through my mind as I run. Our first meeting outside the bar, dancing at the wedding, even a few times when I made her angry. Every moment we've had together has been memorable, but they aren't enough. I want more time with her.

Counting the avenues as I go, I have two more blocks to run. I can see the firetrucks and safety team a block ahead, which means they'll probably stop me.

I break through the barricade and slam into a large man's chest. "You can't be in here."

I struggle to catch my breath but finally get out, "Firefighter… my girlfriend… need to see her."

"She's your girlfriend? I'm sorry, sir, but I can't let you through. They're still trying to rescue her."

That one sentence brings my world crashing in on me. She's one of the two inside. She's the only woman on her crew, so it has to be her. He must assume I got a call.

Adrenaline kicks in and I tear through him, running toward the scene like a crazy person. I have to get to her.

"I don't need anyone to rescue me," Jillian's voice rings out in my head as I push forward, choking on the smoke in the air. Two men grab me before I can get any closer. "Jillian!" I scream out as though she'll answer, pushing against the brute of a man holding me.

A firefighter approaches me with his palms out, telling me to calm down, but I can't focus on him. I need to get to Jillian. "Hold up, Sam. Wait, please."

I concentrate on the face in front of me, and his name registers on my tongue. "Barkley?"

"Yeah, I'd say good to see you again, but I wish it was better circumstances."

I relax, my body giving up the fight. "Is it her?" I ask timidly, hoping he says no. His face doesn't shout "no" though. He's Jillian's best friend on the crew, and her partner. I had hoped momentarily that it meant she's fine since he is, but now I know that's not the case. "Why aren't you with her?"

"She went in before me this time. The captain needed me somewhere else. She's not alone though."

But she's not safe either. He didn't say she's fine or unharmed, just that she's not alone. The thing people fear more than anything is dying alone. Is he trying to tell me she's dying?

I mentally slap myself. I need to avoid jumping to conclusions.

"She's been trapped for a while. They're calling for her

with no luck. Neither she nor Tucker answers."

"She's in there with Tucker?" My voice changes from concern to anger as I remember the moment at the party where he forced her to touch him inappropriately.

"Now isn't a time for jealousy, Sam."

"I'm not jealous. Last night he—" I stop before relaying the story of what happened. At this moment, it seems trivial in comparison. "Never mind, it's not important right now. What are they doing to get her out?"

"Everything possible. As soon as I know anything at all, I'll come over to you. For now though, you have to get behind the barricade. If anything happens to you, Jilli will tear me a new asshole. You feel me?"

"Thanks, Barkley. Please do everything—"

"Man, she's important to me too. And I'd never seen her happier before you came along. She's coming home." He waves at a man behind the barricade who's holding a woman back, calling out, "She's mine. I'll be right there!" Turning his attention back to me, he says, "That's my wife. I need to let her see me up close."

He tugs me along with him so I get behind the barricade while his wife plants kisses all over his face as she cries with joy. I hope I get a moment of relief with Jillian.

While waiting, I call and give everyone the news we feared: Jillian's in trouble. My first call is to Stephan, who arrives about ten minutes later. Together we pace back and forth, hoping for news. I see a reporter getting ready, looking excited, so I step outside to listen.

She puts on a sullen expression like donning a pair of gloves. "Captain Charles Marks is here with me, giving us an update on the rescue efforts."

She shoves the microphone in his face, and his expression is more genuine, though it's also gloomier. I know he considers Jillian to be like his daughter. This must hurt him almost as much as it does me.

"We cleared one area and another piece collapsed in the process. No one else has been trapped, but our people are working diligently to get to their fellow—" He chokes up, and I feel my legs weaken beneath me.

Giving my hand a squeeze, Stephan smiles sadly at me. "She's a fighter. You know this."

All I know right now is I want to scream at the top of my lungs. I wish for Hulk powers so I can tear through the building and carry her out.

She rescued me once. It's my turn now.

What will my life be without her? What was it before her? We've barely been together a few months, but she's already a huge part of my life.

Long away from the real world, in my own zone of emotion, I stay there until arms wrap around me. I feel soft hair against my cheek, a familiar scent of coconut invading my nose, and I sigh. "Jillian?"

But when I open my eyes, Carrie's gazing back at me with misty eyes. "I'm sorry."

"You smell like her. Like coconut."

"She used it in college. I used to borrow it and loved how it smelled. We use the same shampoo. I thought you saw me. Now I realize you're still in shock. She's—"

"A fighter, I know," I snap quicker than I mean to, but

I'm growing tired of the cliché words of encouragement. Nothing will make me feel better except holding her in my arms and hearing her sweet voice say something sarcastic to me.

"We've got one!"

Applause erupts, and my heart stops for at least the tenth time today. Paramedics rush forward with a stretcher, and I see the body of the firefighter being carefully pulled out about fifteen minutes later. It's Tucker.

Holding his hat in his hand, Barkley walks over to me. "They said Jillian insisted he went first. Said he was in worse shape. They had to obey her orders since she's their superior. She's alive though, and talking. That's good news."

The woman I love being alive *is* good news. I love her even more knowing what an unselfish human being she is. Tucker doesn't deserve her kindness, but she put his life first anyway.

"Sam, come with me," Captain Marks says. He leads me to one of the trailers used by the construction company. "I know how close you and Jillian have become. She talks about you quite often. I want to prepare you for something." He points to a seat for me. Unsure my legs will withstand the news, I sit as instructed.

"The good news is she's alive. The bad news is she's in rough shape. They're pulling her out now. After they removed Tucker, she passed out. When they finally reached her, they discovered why. Her leg was pinned beneath a beam, and when they removed it, the pain shot through her system, sending her into shock. Her face is swollen, with lacerations and bruising from the impact."

I can't breathe. I want him to stop talking, but he keeps going. "She's inhaled a lot of soot and dirt into her lungs. It's going to be a long recovery."

Standing up, I start toward the door, but Marks stops me. "They need to get her to the hospital immediately. It's touch and go. There's no time for a reunion with her until she's stable. I pulled you in here so they can get her to the ambulance without interference from you. Do you understand me? You try to go to her and you could be responsible for her death."

"I got it. What hospital?"

"Vanderbilt."

I run out the door and see them loading her into the ambulance. She's so still, and I can't help but stare at her as they lift her up, willing her to move, to feel my presence and acknowledge that I'm here with her, for her. I want to run to her, but the captain's words ring in my ears. I won't be responsible for never hearing her voice again.

With all the strength I have left, I turn to walk the other way, toward Stephan. "Get me to Vanderbilt, now."

"Don't you want to see her?" He must be able to see the turmoil brewing in my eyes, because he reaches in his pocket, pulls out the car keys, and says, "Let's go. I'll drive."

CHAPTER
SIXTEEN

Seven Hours Earlier

I slip on jeans and my station T-shirt, ready to start on my list of errands to run before work begins. I don't have to be in until noon, but at eleven I receive a text stating they need everyone in for a fire with a downtown address. I head to the station and make it in time to get in the third truck leaving. Grabbing my personal protective equipment, I throw it in the truck so I can slip it on as we drive.

A construction site caught fire—usually they're electrical in these cases. Approaching the area, I can see the smoke billowing into the air, as well as flames shooting up and out from different parts of the building. We're the last team on site; everyone else is ready to go.

Captain grabs me as I'm suiting up. "There are construction workers inside. I need you and Tucker to check the south side of the building."

"Yes, sir." I slip on my helmet and follow Tucker, biting my tongue. He isn't my choice for a work partner today, but I've disobeyed orders enough lately.

We head toward the south side of the building and the flames are being extinguished by the first two teams. Tucker and I check out the building for any signs of life. Construction sites not only have workers, but also the occasional squatter who resides there when the workers aren't present. During the summer months, construction happens mostly at night to keep the chances of heatstroke down due to the high temperatures in Nashville; the homeless will take advantage of the site for shade during the day if they find a way in.

Tucker isn't speaking to me, probably because of the hard rejection I gave him last night. I'm perfectly fine with his silence. We enter through the south side as ordered, still able to feel the heat from the fire even though we're away from the flames. This part of the building looks like it suffered a lot of damage. I search the room for signs of life, but there's no one here but us.

Tucker grabs ahold of my arm. My first thought, however irrational, is that he's about to be inappropriate again, so I yank my arm away. He tugs again and pulls me against him, then tries to turn. Before we can get out, the floor above rains down on us. Everything happens so quickly that I don't have time to prepare before Tucker's body falls mostly on me.

I also feel the weight of something else on my leg, most likely a beam.

I push my helmet up and pull the mask off my face as I cough and try to catch my breath. Not the best idea to remove my helmet since the building is unstable, but I can't help feeling claustrophobic. Tucker has a piece of rebar possibly going through his side—I can't see the whole thing to tell the extent of the injury—and his helmet is digging into my chest.

"Tucker," I choke out between coughs. "Tucker, are you alive?" He hasn't moved since we fell. I worry we're both going to die in here.

I keep choking and breathing in the dust around me, but I can't put my mask back on now because of the position I'm in. Tears form in my eyes as I think about Sam. Is this how we end? I should've told him I loved him last night, or this morning— anytime before now.

"Tucker, please." I beg for him to wake up so I'm not alone in this. I'm not sure how much time passes, but finally Tucker groans and tries to shift positions.

"Don't move too much. You're hurt."

"I need to get off you so you can breathe." His attempt to move is futile. He clearly has no strength left.

"I'll be fine," I choke out.

He chuckles softly. "Yeah, you certainly sound fine. Fuck. I feel like a building fell on top of me."

"Don't make me laugh. It's hard enough to breathe already." I can't move my right leg, something's pinning it down. Tucker's on my left, I can tell from the pressure, and I know as soon as he moves I'll feel the extent of my injuries.

I lift my hand to my face to check myself and see fresh blood. "One of us is bleeding."

Tucker knocks his helmet off. "Pretty sure it's me. My side is burning. I'm not going to look. My brain doesn't need to know right now." He lifts his head, and I see his face is covered in scratches and bruises. His mask had been knocked off in the fall, and it must have cut his face in the process.

"Look, Jill, about last night." He swallows hard, his eyes rolling up to meet mine. "I'm sorry. I was a complete jerk and you didn't deserve to be treated that way. I had too much to drink, but it doesn't excuse how I acted."

"I know you weren't yourself. That's why I distracted Sam from beating you up afterward. I appreciate the apology though."

I never felt threatened by Tucker's advances. I may have taken extreme measures to get a point across and because he put my hand on him, but I knew him well enough to know he thought the move had been a seductive one, not a way of forcing himself on me, or else he would have grabbed me instead. Still, him acknowledging he was wrong to assume anything means a lot to me.

Static from the radio sounds, then Barkley's voice is calling my name.

"Where's the radio?" We try looking around for it, and I spot the red light across to my right. "Dammit. It must've fallen when we did. Maybe I can reach it." I try to shift my weight, but we're pinned down together.

"Don't strain yourself. They'll get to us. You know this crew won't let anything happen to you," Tucker tries to reassure me.

"Is that a crack about me being a girl? Because you know I can take care of myself." No one on the crew treats me differently for being a woman, except when it comes to someone treating me badly.

"I know, Hartford. It's what attracts me to you. You're the most badass chick I know." He winks and cringes at the same time. "My face hurts."

"It hurts me too, Tucker."

We both laugh at the jab and then break into a chorus of coughing.

A rumble, followed by a giant crack, sends more rubble down on top of us. Tucker covers my face with his hands, trying to protect me, and part of the ceiling hits his hand, causing him to push down hard on my eye. I'm sure I'll have a bruise, but his action most likely saved me from being blinded permanently. His gloves scratched my face, though I'm grateful for his reflexes. I feel his chest moving against me, but he's unconscious again.

Voices in the distance are calling out to us.

"Help us," I try to shout, but I have little to no volume with all the junk coating my throat. "Tucker, wake up please." I try to push up on him with a nudge, but he's too hard to move.

"Sam," I cry out, my voice cracking with emotion. "Please help me." In reality, he's probably still at the office with clients, not even aware that I'm trapped in this building. But all I can think of is getting out to tell him I love him. If I get out of here, it's the first thing I'm going to do. He may not feel the same, but it's a chance I'm willing to take.

"Sam," I whisper once more as the fear of dying alone sets in. Tucker's here, but he's unconscious, and it's getting harder to breathe with each passing second. I can hear noises in the distance, but it still seems so far away from us.

Moving my hand, I'm able to find Tucker's wrist and keep my fingers on it so I can feel his pulse. There's not much light left, which means the sun has gone down. By now, Sam's at least gotten to my house and is probably visiting with Stephan.

What will he do when I don't show up?

My eyes fight to close while my body fights staying awake. I need to be awake in case they get closer, but the exhaustion overwhelms me, and I drift off. Another rumble, and more debris falls just before I hear voices closer to us.

"Over here," I call out. They're still getting closer but not answering me. "Help us," I call again.

Someone runs over as quickly as they can. I recognize the face now in front of me—his name is Jake. "Hey, Jilli, we're here. We're going to get you out."

"Take Tucker first. But be careful, there's a bar stabbing him. He's been passed out for a while but there's still a pulse." Jake hesitates while checking me over. "Jake, I'm giving you an order." I cough and sputter up more dirt and debris. "Please, get Tucker out of here and come back for me."

The moment they pull him off me, pain shoots through me, and I scream. All the sensations going through my body are too much for me.

The world around me goes black.

CHAPTER
SEVENTEEN

It took them a few hours to stabilize Jillian before they put her in a room. During my waiting period, Stephan, Carrie, Harrison, and Adam all took turns keeping me company. I sent Stephan over to the ER where Adam works to let him know about Jillian, and he came over as soon as his shift ended. We sat in the waiting room in silence. At one point, Adam fixed me a cup of coffee and sat next to me, giving my shoulder a strong grip and patting my back.

I sip on the coffee and send up a few silent prayers that the doctor will be out soon. I haven't set eyes on her since they put her in the ambulance. I need to see her face.

A doctor in dark blue scrubs walks in and heads over

to the desk, speaking to the nurse behind it, who points to Captain Marks. I watch anxiously as the doctor talks with him, wondering what they're discussing, especially when the Captain points over toward me. I stand up as they approach.

Captain Marks turns to the doctor and says, "This is Sam Warner. He's Jillian's significant other. I'd like him to hear what you have to tell me. She'd want him involved."

"You're Jillian's doctor? How is she?"

"I'm Dr. Barrett. She's stable. Her leg was severely crushed. She suffered multiple fractures of the tibia, fibula, and femur on the left side. The orthopedic surgeon is with her now, putting in hardware to piece her leg back together. Her lungs were compromised, so we've got her on oxygen to help with her breathing. As soon as the surgery is complete, you'll be able to see her. If you have any questions, have the nurse at the desk call me. It's going to be a long recovery process, but she's a lucky woman."

Captain Marks steps forward to meet the doctor. "Did you also take care of Tucker Jones?"

The doctor nods and pulls him to the side to speak privately. I see him bow his head and shake it.

As the doctor leaves, I approach the captain. Before I can ask, he tells me, "Tucker didn't make it. The rebar went through his kidney, causing extensive damage. The worst of it was the brain bleed caused by a blow he took to the head. Once it hit him, he was gone. His heart still beat, but his brain had already died before the rescue team found him." He looks up to the ceiling, fighting the tears in his eyes.

"I can tell Jillian for you when she wakes up."

He places his hand on my shoulder and nods. Looking back, I'm glad I didn't tell Barkley the story about what happened at the party. Tucker's life is over, and I don't know how Jillian's going to take it. For all I know, he's the reason she's still alive. If so, I owe him my life.

"How are you holding up, man?" Adam asks. "Wait, stupid question?"

"No. I'm better knowing she's going to be fine. Look, man, you can head home. I know you've been up all night. I'll call you when she's awake."

"I'll go home, get a few hours of shut-eye, and will be back. If you need anything before then, call me." Grabbing my hand, he pulls me in for a hug and pats my back. "Thank you for getting a hold of me."

I send Carrie and Harrison home as well, but Stephan insists on staying. "What's the first thing you're going to say to her when you see her?" he asks me once it's just the two of us.

"The thing I should have said last night. I'm going to tell her how I feel. Last night was the worst night. I've never been so terrified in my life."

"I've known her for several years now. The guy she dated before you was such an ass. I hated to see her hurt when it ended, but I was glad to see him go." He pauses a minute and adds, "I talked to Captain Marks. He tried to contact Jilli's mom, but her number's been disconnected."

"Was she her emergency contact, then?"

"Turns out it was Marks himself. He refused to release

her name to the press because he didn't know how to contact you and didn't want you to find out through the media. He was trying to find your number when you showed up."

Knowing Marks did that makes me smile. It means Jillian talks about me enough for her coworkers to know I'm important to her.

The long hours of waiting, mixed with a range of emotions, are making it impossible to stay focused. When Adam returns, it's been over twenty-four hours since it all began. After talking to me for a minute, he requests a room from the nurse for me to lie down. I want to fight him, but I also need to be awake when I can see Jillian.

My head's barely hit the pillow before I'm off into dreamland. It's not a very restful sleep when the nightmares begin. I keep seeing Jillian in my mind. She's calling for me, begging me to come for her. I can see her struggling to get free, Tucker's body trapping her beneath the rubble. I'm struggling to move him from on top of her. I can see the blood spilling out beneath him. He's too heavy, and she's screaming for more help.

I wake up with a start, sweating profusely and unsure of my surroundings. Once I remember I'm at the hospital, I jump up and run out to the desk. Adam strolls over and grabs my arm before I reach it. "She's not awake, but you can go see her." He leads me down the hallway and stops in front of a door. "I went in to check on her while you slept. She doesn't look like herself. Just be prepared, okay?"

He opens the door, and I draw in a breath when I see her. A mask covers her face for the oxygen. One of her eyes is swollen and purple, and she has a split lip, one leg in a cast, and a bandage around her arm.

"She's okay, right?" I whisper, grasping Adam's hand tightly.

He squeezes back. "Yes. She just needs time to heal." Patting my back, he turns to leave. "If you need me, I'll be around. Just send me a text. I came and checked on you earlier while you were sleeping, programmed my number in your phone, and sent myself a text so I have yours too."

"Thanks, Adam."

As I stand there alone in the room with Jillian, I feel a sense of relief. Moving closer, I swallow back the tears at the sight of all her injuries. Pulling a chair up next to the bed, I take her hand in mine and kiss her palm.

"Hey, beautiful." I stroke her cheek lightly with my finger, never taking my eyes off her. "I'd give anything to see those gorgeous green eyes right now." I rest my head on her hand, closing my eyes. "I love you, Jillian. I need you to wake up so you can hear me say it. I love you."

In movies and books, it always seems to work just by telling someone how you feel. Prince Charming woke up Snow White with a kiss, so I figure what the hell. I lean forward and press my lips lightly to hers. Nothing happens. The doctor told us she'll wake up when she's ready, that I must be patient. Patience is not a virtue of mine.

I lay my head down next to her on the bed and fall asleep.

CHAPTER
EIGHTEEN

I feel something against my hand before I open my eyes. I don't want to look in case it's my worst fear. Worst-case scenario would be I open my eyes and I'm still trapped in the building with Tucker. Something is over my mouth and the air smells cleaner, so I open my eyes to see what's going on. The lights are off, the room lit by the moon outside. I'm in the hospital. There's someone next to the bed; I can see the back of their head. I recognize the hair, know it's my Sam, that he came for me. I move my fingers through his hair, stroking it, enjoying the soft feel of it against my skin.

I let a tear fall as I touch him again, something I never thought I'd get to do. "Sam," I try to say, but it sticks in my throat. It's night, so I'm assuming it's been a long day for him and he's exhausted. But selfishly, I need to see his face, hear his voice, look into his bright blue eyes. "Sam," I say a little louder, though it's muffled behind this mask. I lift my hand to remove the mask and rub his shoulder, trying to get his attention.

Lifting his head, he turns to face me. He's groggy, but soon his eyes focus on me. I watch his eyelids open fully, and a smile fills his face. "Baby, how long have you been awake?"

"Just a few minutes." My voice is scratchy from a sore throat. "Water?"

Sam holds a finger up and runs out the door. He returns a few minutes later.

"They gave me ice chips for you." Taking a large piece of ice between his fingers, he rubs it lightly across my lips, wetting them and letting the moisture fall into my mouth. "Maybe you can pretend we're in a sexier setting as I do this?" He grins and grabs another piece of ice. "I have been so worried about you. I wanted to be awake when you opened your eyes."

"It's been a long day, I guess?"

"Two long days, almost three. They rescued you over twenty-four hours ago."

Holy crap, I've lost two days already? "Tucker?"

"You probably shouldn't talk. You need rest." I've been resting long enough, in my opinion. All I want to do is look at Sam. "There's something I want to tell you."

"Tell me about Tucker, please. Is it bad? He saved my life."

"What do you mean?" Sam asks.

So I tell him all about the way Tucker protected me when the building collapsed. All about his apology and the way he covered my face when the second collapse happened. His face tells me something is very wrong.

"Is Tucker paralyzed?" He shakes his head but avoids my question. "Tell me, Sam, please."

"He didn't make it, Jillian. I'm sorry."

"What? No, that's not possible. How? Was it his wound?" I remember the rebar being through his side. My first assumption is it went through an organ.

"They said it was a brain bleed. He wasn't in pain. The impact ruptured arteries in his head and he never felt anything after. By the time he made it to the hospital, there was nothing they could do."

We'd been talking until the second collapse. He covered my face, and in the process, the chunk of concrete meant for me hit him in the head instead. It should have been me.

Panic rises in my chest and I start gasping for air, having a full attack. Sam hits the button for the nurse, then runs to the door and calls for help. They send him outside while they work to calm me.

I fight against the pain, against the machines, against anyone trying to help me. Tears stream down my face as I sob for my friend. *He was only twenty-three. He didn't deserve to die.*

The nurse tries to hold me down, but I want out of this bed. Fighting against her, I feel a prick in my arm and I drift into unconsciousness again.

CHAPTER
NINETEEN

"What happened?" Grabbing my arm, Adam pulls me away from the door so the doctors can get inside. "Did she wake up?"

"Yeah. She found out about Tucker and had a panic attack."

"What? You told her about Tucker? She's too weak for such news." No one is angrier at me than I am with myself right now.

"Like I don't know that?" I step closer, getting in his face. "It was the first thing she wanted to know. I don't lie too well, which is a good quality most days. What was I supposed to say when she asked me about him?"

Placing a hand on each of my shoulders, Adam pulls me into a hug. "I'm sorry. I probably would've done the same thing."

The doctors and nurses clear the room, and Dr. Barrett steps over to me. "She's been sedated. No visitors for the rest of the evening." I open my mouth to argue, and he holds up a finger. "No exceptions. She needs her rest to heal. You can sit outside her room—hell, you can stare at her through the window for all I care—but you step one foot in that room before I okay it and I'll have you thrown out. Do you hear me?"

"Thank you, Doctor. I'll be right here."

"No, you won't. You haven't eaten in days. She's asleep. Let's go to the cafeteria." Adam doesn't let me argue either, especially after my stomach growls with the need for food.

The smells assault my nose when we step through the cafeteria doors. I reach for a sandwich and Adam stops me. "Go for the pizza. It's baked daily, whereas that sandwich could've been packaged a week ago. You don't need food poisoning on top of everything else going on."

Two giant slices of pizza and soda—not the healthiest meal, but who cares. We sit at a table and neither of us speaks for a few minutes.

"Did Jillian ever tell you how we met?" Adam asks, and I shake my head.

"I was on night shift in the ER. She'd come in on a stretcher. A child was trapped in their home, and she was inside too long trying to save her. She suffered heat exhaustion as well as smoke inhalation. The child survived though, thanks to her."

The fact that she always puts everyone's life ahead of hers is admirable, but incredibly frustrating when you're someone who cares so deeply for her.

"I went in to check on her before I left for the evening, I was having a rough night myself. EJ's sister and niece had been in an accident. It was before we started officially dating, but I was already head over heels in love with him. She made the mistake of telling me I looked sad and asked if everything was okay. I pulled up a chair and spent the evening talking to her about my feelings for him. She gave me great advice about love. The problem with Jilli is she knows how to make everyone else feel better, but has no clue how to use her own advice." He sets his food down and takes a deep breath. "She's going to push you away."

"How do you know?" I push my plate aside. "Well, it doesn't matter because I won't let her."

"Good. You need to be strong. You're going to be forced to fight for her. She's going to push hard, probably treat you badly, hitting sore spots to dig in deeper. If you love her—"

"I do, no question." Nothing means more to me than Jillian. I'll give my own life for her if that's what it takes.

"Good, then you can't stop until she lets you back in."

It's as though Adam can predict the future, because everything happens the way he said it would. The doctor never let me back in the room. The moment Jillian woke up, she gave them a list of the only visitors she wanted, and I'm not on it. For a week, I sit outside her door, relying on the visitors who come out to know how she is. They all try to convince her to see me, but she refuses to budge.

Discharge day comes, and the nurse puts her in a wheelchair and escorts her out of the room. I stand with a smile on my face when she comes out looking more like the woman I love. The swelling on her face is down and her lip is healing. The long leg cast will take getting used to, but other than that, she looks amazing.

Her eyes don't reach mine, and the nurse mouths her apology as she passes by. The rejection stings, so much so that I wonder if Adam is wrong about one thing.

I'm starting to doubt that Jillian will ever want me again.

Being her neighbor, Stephan offers to pick Jillian up from the hospital and take her home. He's done a few things to help around her house, like building a removable ramp on the porch to help with the wheelchair for as long as needed. He also rearranged her cabinets to make things easier to reach.

I pick up a few things, including flowers, before driving over to see her. Stephan answers the door. "Hey, man," he says as he steps out the door. "She doesn't want to see you."

"I know. I thought maybe you needed to pick up something at your house. You could accidentally leave the door open and I could stroll in. She can't blame you for it." Putting my palms together, I silently beg him.

He ponders it a moment, looks over his shoulder, and nods. "Jilli, I'll be right back. I have to grab something at home."

"Okay," she yells from inside. I close the door behind me as I step in the house. "That was quick," she says before looking up and noticing it's me. A small smile graces her lips briefly before it turns to a scowl. "What do you want?"

"Just to see you. To talk for a moment." It takes a lot of strength, but I keep my distance from her. Just having her talk to me is a breakthrough.

"I'm sure you have better things to do," she snaps.

I throw the flowers down, frustration taking over. "Give me a break, Jillian. You've been in the hospital for a week, and I've been there. I never left! From the minute I saw the news about the fire, all I've wanted to do is hold you in my arms. I've barely eaten since it happened. I haven't been to work. I took showers in the hospital. Today is the first day I've had something other than scrubs on." My voice switches from angry to pleading. "Stop pushing me away and look at me."

She starts to cry. "Tucker was twenty-three. It's my fault he died, Sam. I don't deserve to be happy."

"No, it's not your fault." I bend down in front of her chair, taking her hand.

"He was awake and speaking to me. There was a second collapse. When we heard it start, he placed his hands and head over mine to protect me. The chunk of concrete that killed him was meant for me. I shouldn't be alive."

In my mind, I see her body lying lifeless on the stretcher. I hear the doctor telling me that she didn't make it because of a brain bleed. I couldn't have handled those words.

"Don't say things like that, please."

She pulls her hand away. "Why do you care?"

Tears glisten in her eyes. I see so much pain in them that it breaks my heart.

"Jillian, when I found out you were the one trapped, I couldn't breathe. I felt a pain I'd never experienced in my life. I thought I'd never see those beautiful green eyes of yours again. That I'd never laugh at one of your sarcastic comments, never hear you call me Sammy again."

She sucks her lips between her teeth, her forehead creasing. I see her body shake as the tears fall, and I reach up to wipe them away. Caressing her cheek, I whisper, "You should know by now how I feel about you."

"I think I need you to say it, just to be sure… Sammy."

With my hands pressed against her face, I lean forward to brush my lips against hers. She doesn't resist, so I push further, letting my tongue slip between her lips. I missed the taste of her. Her hands move to my shirt, slipping underneath to slide up my skin. "Tell me, please," she whispers against my mouth.

"I love you, Jillian Nonexistent Hartford."

Erupting with laughter, another thing I missed, she says, "I love you too, Samuel Linus Warner." Peering up at me, she asks, "I'm so sorry for pushing you away. Will you stay with me tonight?"

"I'd hoped you'd ask. So much that I stopped by Harrison's to get an overnight bag before I came. It's in the car." Kissing her forehead, I rise to my feet again. "I'll run out and get it."

"And you can tell Stephan that things went fine in

the process. He doesn't have to come back tonight. And thank him for not listening to me… this time, at least."

I practically skip next door, where I find Stephan sitting on his porch. "Did it work?"

"Yep. She asked me to stay the night. And she isn't mad at you for not listening to her. Her words." I see the relief wash over him. "Come over tomorrow for lunch, maybe?"

"Do you not have to work?"

"I've taken a leave of absence for a while. My brother is going to call me on an as-needed basis, but for now, I'm focused on helping Jillian."

"Damn glad she has you, man. Ask her to tell you about Jeff sometime. You'll see why I'm so happy you're around." He pats my shoulder. "Call me if you need anything."

When I walk back into Jillian's, she's sitting patiently, waiting for me to return. "Can I help you get to the couch or something?" I offer.

"I was hoping you'd carry me to bed. I've been sleeping so much lately, but I'm still exhausted."

She places her arm around my neck, and I put one arm behind her back, the other under her good leg, and lift. The weight of the cast makes it awkward to carry her, but I manage to get her to the bedroom. I turn sideways, careful not to bang her leg against the door, and set her on the bed.

"This may be the wrong time to ask, but Stephan mentioned Jeff? You brought him up once before but didn't say much." The moment I say his name she tenses up, and I see a vulnerability rarely visible on Jillian's face. "If you don't want to talk about it, I'll understand."

"I don't like speaking his name or thinking about him, but you've told me everything about Anya, so it seems only fair you know about my ex." I take a seat next to her on the bed as she speaks. "Jeff and I dated for three years, but that part I told you I suppose. The two of you are polar opposites, which is what I love most about you. He would complain about me." She pauses.

"Complain about you how?"

"My size, I've never been a single-digit wearing woman." Her curves are some of my favorite things about her. I love how soft her skin is and how she isn't afraid to eat what she enjoys. "He kept track of our sex life and would get mad when we went more than two days without it. And then when we had sex, he would jump up and clean himself off. There was no cuddling after. He wanted it on demand but acted as though it was taking up too much of his time."

I lean over and nuzzle my nose against her cheek. "He doesn't know what he missed out on. I love my Jillian cuddles." She giggles, and her shoulder rises as she tries to push away from the tickling of my skin against hers.

"He tried to take away my self-confidence and my trust, and he almost succeeded. And somehow I thought I was in love with him back then." I expect to see tears, but she's much stronger than most. He didn't succeed in damaging her because she didn't allow him to.

"I don't know how you put up with him for as long as you did."

"In the beginning he was sweet, for a few months at least. The verbal abuse wasn't noticeable at first, not to me at least. He made it seem like jokes, so I laughed it off. Later it became more hurtful, and when I opened up to Stephan about him, he talked sense into me."

"I think I've heard enough to know I hate the guy. Let's change the subject, agreed?" If I have to hear any more about this guy, I'll probably search him out just to punch him in the face. Of course I could also thank him for being such a jerk and saving Jillian for me.

"Can you help me undress so I can be comfortable?"

Such an innocent question in this situation, but my brain—and other parts—don't see it that way. I swallow, lick my lips, and try to think of anything but her naked body as I lift her shirt over her head. Grabbing a tank top out of the drawer, I turn back to see she's removed her bra with one hand. She doesn't bother to cover herself, and my body instantly reacts to hers no matter how I try to stop it.

Taking a seat next to her on the bed, I lift the tank top, and she pushes it away, taking my hand and placing it on her breast instead. "I need to feel you touch me."

Cupping her breasts, I watch her eyes close as her mouth makes an O when my thumbs flick against her nipples. Dipping my head down, I take one in my mouth, swirling my tongue around the tip. She gasps and begs for me to suck harder, and I happily oblige. My need for her is fierce, reflected in my kiss when I move up to her face again. Forgetting the last few days, I move to lay her back on the bed, and she winces in pain.

"I'm sorry. We shouldn't—"

She presses her lips to mine again, making me forget

what I want to say, she shifts her body, using both hands to raise her casted leg onto the bed before she lies down. I crawl around the bed to hover over her. My first kiss goes to her forehead, then to her cheek, and her chin. I avoid her mouth as I explore her skin. She tugs on her shorts, so I ease them down her body, over her cast, and onto the floor. She's lying in only a pair of panties, and I gaze at her body. The bruises are fading but still there. I bend to gently kiss the areas around her injuries so as not to cause her pain.

"Take your clothes off." Her assertiveness is quite the turn-on. She's making it increasingly difficult to stop this from going too far.

"Yes, ma'am."

I lift the T-shirt over my head, enjoying the way Jillian watches me, the heat of her stare warming me from head to toe as I remove my jeans. Lying down beside her, I move as close to her as possible. I wish she could turn on her side so I could settle behind her, but the cast keeps her on her back.

"As much as I want this, and believe me I do, I think we should wait." The words taste bitter on my tongue because I don't want to wait to be with her, but I don't want to hurt her either.

"But you'll stay in here with me?"

She sits up, and I pull the tank over her head, then lay my head on her shoulder and my arm across her waist. Lying here with her feels good. It's so comforting that the last week catches up with me quickly and I fall fast asleep.

Jillian hasn't moved when I wake up. Terror grips my chest and I shake her until her eyes open.

"What's wrong?" She rubs her eyes groggily.

I sigh in relief. "I'm sorry. I got scared."

"I'm fine, Sammy. You're not getting rid of me so easily."

"Getting rid of you is the last thing I want to do." I place a kiss on her nose and jump up out of bed. "I'll go grab your wheelchair if you're ready to get up."

"Yes, I'm ready. I'm starving too."

"I'll order us dinner."

I place a call for Chinese takeout before grabbing the chair. As I'm heading back to her room, I hear a thud and Jillian cries out in pain. I leave the chair to rush to her side where she's sprawled on the floor next to her bed.

I reach down to help her, and she slaps my hand away. "Leave me alone!"

She's crying as I lie next to her on the ground.

"I'm not going anywhere, Jillian. Stop fighting me." Staring at whatever is behind me, she refuses to make eye contact. "You can ignore me, hit me, whatever you need to heal, but I'm not leaving. I'm in love with you, and nothing is going to change the way I feel."

"Why?" This time our eyes meet. "What makes me so great?"

"Everything." I roll over on my side, propping myself up on my elbow. "Since the moment my drunk ass called you Betty, I've loved you. I just didn't know it at the time. I came to tell you the day you were having the party. We got interrupted every time I tried."

"You weren't the only one scared to never see someone again. I thought about you the whole time I was trapped in the building, Tucker dying on top of me. I can't get his face out of my mind." Her sobs are breaking my heart. I feel helpless to ease her pain. "I hate not being able to do things for myself, which makes me feel selfish because he's dead. He can't do anything anymore, and I'm mad that I can't have sex with my boyfriend."

"Stop beating yourself up. Tucker wouldn't want you to do that. I didn't know him, but hearing what he did for you down there tells me he was a good guy."

Watching her cry, the blame she feels, seeing the guilt eating away at her, I know I have to find a way to help her.

CHAPTER TWENTY

JILLIAN

If I didn't love Sam before the accident, I would fall for him now for sure. He's never given up on me. He's being so patient with the lack of sex, constantly caring for me, making sure I'm taking my medicines on time. He downloaded an app just to be sure he knows when I take what and how much.

I'm still not sure what I did to deserve him, but I'll do it again to keep him around. My emotions have been all over the place. At times, I want to leave my own body and never come back. He must love me as much as he says, or he would've left weeks ago with my mood swings.

I have him take a sleeping pill so he can get some rest.

After much coaxing, he finally succumbs to my demands. Throughout the night, he tosses and turns, mumbling incoherently. I can't sleep, so I watch him. My name slips from his lips, and the next moment he sits up, violently thrashing in the covers while screaming for me. I sit up to calm him, but his eyes don't open. Hugging him tightly, I hold on while he screams. Whatever he's dreaming must change in some way, because he falls limp in my arms, and I soon hear him snoring in my ear.

Rolling him over, I whisper, "I hope you have sweeter dreams." I kiss his cheek and move away again.

Turning over to face me, he throws his hand on top of me. I giggle when he moves it up and cups my breast.

"Nice move, Sammy. It's not nice to pretend to sleep." His lips form a grin. "How long have you been faking it?"

"Heard you whisper in my ear." His hand remains on my boob.

"You were thrashing around pretty badly. Bad dream?"

He shrugs and says, "Don't remember," but I see in his eyes that he does.

I don't press him for answers, especially when he rolls over and kisses me. It's all we do lately is kiss and fool around a bit. My body aches for him, but he worries it's too soon. It's been eight weeks and counting since we last had sex. Believe me, I'm counting.

I can feel his want for me against my leg. As he kisses me, I move my hand down to stroke him. He groans against my mouth. "Slow. It's been a while."

I feel the wetness pool between my thighs because he

hasn't let me get this far in a while. I pump him slowly, hoping he'll want to be inside me. His fingers find my center and I gasp.

"God, you're so wet."

"Please don't stop," I beg him. He reaches next to me and opens the drawer in the nightstand. I grin when I see him pull out a condom. *Victory!* "Thank you," I whisper, making him chuckle.

Rolling the condom on quickly, he presses himself against my core and slowly slides inside me. A long, breathy sigh of contentment flows from me. It's not even about sex right now. We both need this moment of closeness, to be together without anything else between us. No memories, no heartache, no worries—just raw, naked pleasure. Since it's been a while, it doesn't take either of us long to reach our peaks, both gasping for air as we come back down.

"I love you," Sam whispers before pulling out and lying beside me. He snuggles his head against my shoulder. "Can we stay in bed today?"

Before I can answer, he's snoring again.

"I guess so," I say with a chuckle, then lie down beside him, falling asleep easily.

A few hours later, the alarm on the phone goes off, reminding me it's time to take my medicine.

Sam sits up, wiping the grogginess from his eyes, and checks the clock. "I can't believe I slept so late."

"You wanted to stay in bed, so who cares?"

"I did? No, I have errands to run today. I need to get—" He stops and looks down at the condom still on his cock.

"What the hell?" His eyes widen and he stares at me, then back down at the condom.

I sit up, pulling the sheet over me. "Oh my God. You slept through it? That was the sleeping pills, wasn't it?" Smacking my palm against my forehead, I groan. "You told me you've walked out of the apartment naked before. I didn't know you could have sex without realizing it. Which is a bit concerning, honestly."

"We had sex and I missed it?" He drops his head back down onto the pillow.

"If it makes you feel better, you were amazing as always. I feel like a pervert now though." What else would you call a person who has sex with someone who's asleep? Our moment of bliss is tainted now.

"I've never had this happen before. I'm so sorry, Jillian." Grabbing the bottle of pills off the nightstand, he tosses them in the wastebasket. "I'm not taking those again. Ever."

"I'm up for showing you what you missed, if you are?"

After checking the clock, and seemingly calculating a few things in his head, he nods. While he might have slept through our first encounter, I didn't, and I will enjoy recreating it for him.

Sam gets me settled on the couch before he leaves to run errands. A few minutes later, Stephan arrives like clockwork. The two have their schedules synced. "Someone is glowing," Stephan comments. "You got laid?"

Normally I'm not one to kiss and tell the full details, but

I share my embarrassment with Stephan, who enjoys a good full belly laugh at my expense. "It's not my fault. Those pills are crazy!"

"I feel bad for Sam missing out."

"After I explained it to him, I gave him a replay, which went even better." He offers me a high five. "Can you make us some lunch? I'm starving."

His idea of making lunch is ordering Chinese takeout. While we wait, I start a conversation I've been wanting to have for a while. "How is work?"

"It's going great. I sold apps to six more schools."

"Are you still unhappy with your accountants?"

"Yeah, they're too stuffy. Are you considering my offer after all these years?"

"If you're still offering, I'd like to."

"What about the firehouse?"

"I'm resigning." Before he can lecture me, I hold up my hand and explain. "I know what you're going to say. I do love my job, but I can't do it anymore. Not right now, at least. It's getting too hard. The people I can't save, Tucker, everything."

"What about the ones you do save? Like Sam?"

"Sam's the best thing that's ever happened to me. I've seen how this has affected him too, and I don't want to hurt him anymore. He's struggling with it as much as I am."

Stephan doesn't hesitate, holding his hand out. "The job is yours."

We shake on it, and I pull his hand forward until he hugs me.

CHAPTER
TWENTY-ONE

For two months, I sleep in the bed, cuddling with Jillian. Waiting on her hand and foot is easy; the mood swings are the hard part. It's the end of October, the weather cooling off a little, and she's been getting out of the house more. I make sure to get her out at least three times a week, though some days it takes more convincing than others.

Day to day becomes a constant teeter-totter of emotions. One minute she's laughing with me and making jokes, and the next she's in tears, criticizing herself for feeling any joy. No matter what I say, I'm hopeless in convincing her that she isn't responsible for Tucker's death.

Captain Marks insists she see a therapist before returning

to work in the future, but I haven't convinced her to start yet. I'm hoping after a few weeks of physical therapy, she'll agree to some mental therapy. My goal is to have her feeling better in time for our first Christmas together.

The cast recently came off, so she's now participating in physical therapy every day. I've been working on call for Harrison when a client needs to see a house. Since I screwed up and booked a client to see a house at the same time as her doctor's appointment, I have to ask Stephan to take her for me. We've been sharing the responsibility like an estranged couple sharing custody.

My insurance money for the apartment came through, but I've put off looking for a place while I take care of Jillian. I have ulterior motives as well. During some of my time alone, when I can get online or after showing a house, I've been looking at rings, though I want to wait until she's healed—at least physically—before I ask. It scares me to think that she may never heal fully from Tucker's loss.

"Sam?" she calls out from the other room.

"Be right there, honey." I've been trying out pet names, but they don't roll off my tongue very smoothly. "What are you doing?" I ask as I walk into the room. Jillian is on the floor, crawling toward me. "Where are your crutches?" The doctor recommended she use crutches, even without the cast, until her muscles get stronger with therapy.

"Just lift me up, please."

I place both arms beneath hers and lift, laying her down gently on the bed. She sighs dramatically, throwing an arm over her face.

"What is that smell?"

She lifts her arm just enough to speak. "Vomit."

"Oh. The pain pills are still making you sick?"

Sitting up a bit, she explains, "No, I stopped taking them. I don't know what it is now. I called the doctor and he says he'll reevaluate my meds when I come in to see if that's the cause or if it's some underlying issue."

"Where is this—oh." The vomit is all over the floor on the other side of the bed. "I'll clean it up."

"No! I was trying to get to it myself. I don't want you cleaning up that kind of thing. It's disgusting. You'll never have sex with me again."

"Trust me, it would take a lot more than vomit to make me not want you." I consider my words and add, "Don't do more than vomit though, because some things shouldn't be shared."

She sticks her tongue out at me, and it reminds me of the first time we met officially, at Harrison's wedding.

I make sure she's comfortable before going into the other room to get supplies to clean it up. Thankfully her bedroom has hardwood floors, so it only takes some paper towels and a mop. I don't let her see me gag, but when I go to dispose of the towels, I dry heave a little.

"Let me see if I can get Harrison to cover this client and I'll come with you."

Jillian places her hand on mine. "Please don't. You've sacrificed so much time for me these last few weeks. Stephan will take me to this appointment. I'll call you as soon as it's over."

As much as I want to stay with Jillian, I did make a promise to my brother. He's been working extra-long hours to cover me lately, costing him time with his new wife. Although, Daphne tells me Carrie comes by for lunch every day now and is there for over an hour. Translation: I need to disinfect my desk each time I go to the office.

Glancing at my watch, I notice I'm supposed to meet my client in a half hour, which is how long it takes to get to the address. Giving Jillian a quick kiss goodbye, I run out the door, waving at Stephan as our paths cross.

On the way across town, I make a few calls. Bluetooth headsets are fantastic for multitasking. I arrive five minutes late, but luckily my client isn't there yet.

My text alert goes off.

Jillian: Leaving for the dr now. If you beat me back home, don't eat. I've got something planned for you.

Me: I'm intrigued. Don't overdo it though.

Jillian: I won't. Stephan's helping.

My client comes as I'm smiling at her text, and I put the phone away. "Bill, how are you?"

"Good, Sam. Let's do this final walk-through so I can sign off on my wife's dream house."

"A man with a plan. Makes it easy on me." Bill is part owner of a restaurant chain in town. Two weeks ago, he spotted this house on the market and put a hefty down payment on it. He offered a stipend if they closed quickly too.

Walking through the house, we make note of any issues needing to be cleared up, which are minimal. Since our last inspection, it seems one of the rooms developed a flicker, so we'll need to get an electrician out to check it.

"I'll pay whatever. Get him out here in the next few minutes. I'm not leaving until we know."

Great. I was hoping this would go smoothly so I could meet Jillian at the doctor, but that won't be happening anytime soon. First, I have to call the seller and make sure they'll reimburse my client for the repairs. After taking care of that part, I call the electrician to get him out as soon as possible. He has an opening today. On any other day, I'd be happy to get it out of the way quickly, but I just want to be with Jillian.

"The electrician says he can be here in another hour or so. Do you want to go grab a bite to eat? My treat?" He shakes his head. "Coffee?"

"Nope. I want to stay right here."

Just where I want to spend my day, in an empty house with an uptight businessman. For the next hour and a half, I try to make conversation, but we have less than nothing in common.

Finally, the electrician arrives. After a short while, he tell us, "There's a short in the wiring. I used my handy dandy machine here to check the rest and they seem fine. I'll get this room replaced and you two can be on your way."

While twiddling my thumbs and waiting on the technician, I text Jillian to see if she's still at the doctor.

Me: I'm still stuck with the client. Have you seen the doctor yet?

Jillian: Yes. Too much to type. Talk over dinner. <3

Me: <3

Too much to type? That doesn't sound good. I'm too impatient for this, so I call Jillian, but she doesn't answer. My next call is to Stephan.

"Hey, man, just dropped Jillian off at your house."

"What happened with the doctor? Is she okay?"

"Don't know. She wouldn't tell me anything." I can almost hear his shrug with his reply.

"How did she seem?"

"She came out crying, said he had her do some range of motion tests and such and they caused her some pain."

Sounds believable enough. "Thanks again for taking her. I'll be home in a bit, and I'll call you when dinner's ready."

"Thanks, but I told Jillian I have a date tonight." Translation: He's getting laid.

"Enjoy your night, then."

I disconnect the call and check the time. This freaking electrician is going to drive me insane if he doesn't finish up soon. Heading over to him, I try to keep as much irritation out of my tone as I can manage, which honestly isn't much. "Any chance you're almost done?"

"Yep. Just finished." He flips the switch and the light shines perfectly without any glitches.

"Fantastic." I shake his hand, Bill writes him a check, and we all get to go home. I chat with Bill for a moment regarding a few last-minute instructions and politely wave as he drives off so I don't seem in too much of a hurry.

Once he's out of sight, I drive like I'm racing in the Indy 500, knocking ten minutes off my drive by hitting backroads to avoid the rush-hour traffic on the interstate.

When I run inside, Jillian's lying on the couch with her feet up. "Hey, babe. How did it go with the client?"

"Fine. Had an electrical issue, but we got it fixed. Tell me about the doctor."

"Take off your coat, loosen your tie, and come sit down first." She doesn't appear upset, so I decide to follow her instructions.

Suit jacket on the rack, tie ripped from my neck, I unbutton the two top buttons as I reach the couch. She moves her feet so I can sit next to her. "What did he say?"

She takes my hand. "Calm down. He said he didn't think anything went wrong with the surgery. My range of motion is getting better. There's no sign of infection. He ran a few tests and they came back clean."

I breathe a sigh of relief. "So is it the medicine?"

"He did tell me not to take the pain pills anymore. I told him I stopped them a while ago and only take them as needed. There's something else I want to talk to you about."

"What is it?"

"After my appointment, I had Stephan run me by the firehouse. I turned in my notice to Captain Marks."

"What? Why? Is it your leg? Does the doctor think it won't heal right?" My hand is on the table, and she places hers on top.

"The X-rays show the fractures are healing well, though I've still got about four months of recovery before they'll be completely healed. Plus about three months for the other issue he found today. So I talked to Stephan, and he wants to hire me as a personal accountant for his company. I can work from home, utilize my actual degree, and in a few years, I might try being a volunteer firefighter."

I'm still lost on where this is all coming from.

"I've got four more months of therapy before I can get back on the rotation again. I have to be at 100 percent before I can enter a building." She points at her purse on the table. "Hand me that, please."

The issue she glossed over has me curious, but since she doesn't seem upset, I reach for her purse and pass it to her as she continues. "Stephan's been hounding me to be his personal accountant for years. He uses a company, but they take a percentage and he'd rather have someone he trusts. He's been having me double-check their numbers periodically anyway. I can work for him from home, which will give us more time together."

"Go back. What other issue did he find?"

"Oh, this one." She hands me a slip of paper she pulled from her purse.

"Is this what I think it is?"

"Remember at the party that night? The way we christened Stephan's table?" How could I forget? I nod, urging her to go on. "We didn't use protection because I was on the pill. Well, I take my pill before bed and I forgot in that night. Then the accident happened, and I haven't taken it since."

I look up at her, holding back my smile before I verify her news. "We're having a baby?"

My smile breaks through as I say it aloud and my body relaxes. "Two months?" She nods. "You're due around June?" Again, she nods.

My lips crash into hers, and she laughs against my lips as I say, "I love you," over and over.

"You're gonna be a daddy. I hope you're ready for it."

The elation hits, but I stop, one more question on my mind. "But the accident, all the drugs, the—"

"Our baby is fine. The doctor had me checked out. There's a strong heartbeat, and you'll be able to see it at my next appointment." She takes a deep breath. "How do you feel?"

"There are no words." Nothing verbal could express the amount of happiness I feel. It's my second chance at fatherhood, this time with the right woman by my side.

"Marry me."

"If you don't stop fake proposing to me, one day I'm going to accept."

She doesn't understand that I am completely serious this time.

Getting down on one knee, I take her hand in mine. "Marry me, Jillian."

She shakes her head. "We're not getting married just because there's a baby on the way. You don't have to do that."

"I'm not. Stay here." I walk over to my suit jacket and pull the velvet box out of my pocket. Her hands fly up to cover her nose and mouth, her eyes sparkling with what I hope are happy tears.

"I picked this up from the jeweler today. It's been sized and everything. I planned to go all out, but who needs that? You just gave me the best news of my life. So… marry me?"

"Yes."

CHAPTER
TWENTY-TWO

JILLIAN

When Sam and I met last June, I never could imagine that by Christmas we would be engaged and expecting a baby. Once the ring is on my finger, I insist he move in permanently. By mid-November, he's painting the third bedroom, readying it to be a nursery. Neither of us worry about the traditional pink or blue, since we're not traditional people. Instead, we opt for a *Star Wars* theme for the nursery.

Back on my feet now, without the need for crutches or a walker, I can help get things ready too. I start working for Stephan, making my hours the same as Sam's so we can have time together in the evenings.

Sitting here working on straightening out Stephan's books,

I'm getting a headache. The disorganization of his former accountant is astounding. Saved by the bell, I answer the door. "Captain Marks, come in."

"You can call me Charles now, Jillian."

"No I can't, that's too weird. Would you like some coffee?" He follows me into the kitchen, and I pour him a tall mug—black, no sugar, just the way he likes it.

"What brings you by?" I sip on my cup of coffee with caramel creamer added.

"Wanted to see how you were doing."

"I'm good. I miss you guys."

"We miss you too. It doesn't smell as nice around there as it used to." He chuckles. I always made sure we had air freshener on hand because men in that much gear, especially during the summer months, smell rank. "Would you consider coming back in a couple of months as a volunteer?"

"It would probably be almost a year before I can do that."

We aren't telling everyone about the baby yet; only Stephan knows so far. We plan to tell the rest of the family at Christmas.

"Why so long? You seem to be walking well."

"Well, the baby will be here in June, and then I want a few months at home at least."

Captain Marks is in the middle of a sip of coffee when he stops. His eyes meet mine, and I see a smile forming on his lips.

I give him one in return. "You're one of the first to know. And Sam and I are getting married."

He sets the mug down, stands up, and wraps his arms

around me. For as many years as we've known each other, I haven't gotten many hugs from him, but it's always nice. He's the closest thing I've had to a father in a long time.

"Congratulations, Jilli. I'm so happy for you, darlin'." He pulls away and kisses my cheek. "You're like a daughter to me, you know that?"

"Which brings me to another matter. We haven't made many wedding plans yet because we're going to wait until the baby is here, but I'd like you to walk me down the aisle."

"I'd be honored."

CHAPTER
TWENTY-THREE

One Year Later

The wedding is just a few weeks away, and Jillian and I are working on finalizing the outfits. The only thing we haven't come to an agreement on yet is what Jyn, our daughter, will be wearing.

"Jyn is barely six months old. If you want a *Star Wars*-themed wedding, you have to forgo the flower girl carrying a lightsaber. She'll never be able to hold it."

"I think she could handle it, literally." I bend down to kiss the top of Jyn's head and squeeze her cheeks. Her chubby cheeks push up with a smile. Staring at her Yoda onesie, I come up with an idea. "I can carry her on my back like Luke did."

"You're not dressing like Luke though. Fictional or not, I'm not marrying my brother." Pulling one side of her bottom lip in between her teeth, she says, "Don't hate me, but what if we just elope? This seems like a lot of expense for a wedding."

The cost is getting higher than we budgeted for a few months ago. Perhaps I did get a little carried away. "I at least want our friends and family there."

"Let's compromise. A maid of honor and a best man, dressed as Chewbacca and C-3PO. The rest will be guests. We'll dress as Han and Leia, put Jyn in an R2-D2 dress. What do you think?" She's biting her lip again, as she does when she's unsure of how I will respond.

"I think I love you even more."

The day arrives, and the setup is perfect. Captain Marks even agrees to walk Jillian down the aisle dressed as Darth Vader. Stephan stands up for Jillian, proud to wear a C-3PO outfit. My brother reluctantly dons the Chewbacca outfit, thanking me repeatedly for getting married in the winter. Carrie bought a BB-8 dress from a local store to wear while she kept a hold on Jyn for us during the ceremony. Her dress poofs out just right for the droid with her eight-month pregnancy bump underneath.

We stick to traditional vows, though we do use each other's middle names in them. There is a wave of muttering when I call her Jillian Nonexistent Hartford, but the two of us get the reference so we grin at each other while the rest of the group remains confused.

At the reception, Captain Marks stands up and breathes heavily into the microphone to get everyone's attention. The room erupts in laughter at his Vader impression. His speech has the girls, and even some of the guys, in tears.

He removes the helmet to give the speech. "Jillian, we met five years ago. You walked into the station and, admittedly, I thought, 'This girl will never make it as a firefighter.' You proved me wrong after the first fire when you saved one of our largest men. After that day, I'd correct anyone who said you were less for being a woman. And through the years, as we grew closer, I came to love you like the daughter I always wanted. When I met Sam over here—" He pauses, glances up at Jillian, and winks. "—we were rescuing him from an alien invasion."

Again, the room erupts in laughter—all except for me, sinking down in my chair a little instead. "Thanks, Captain," I mumble. Jillian grasps my hand.

"When Jillian first told me about Sam, I was skeptical. I knew if he ever hurt her he'd have to answer to me." A chorus of "And me" rings out from the crowd from several of her crew. Barkley even cracks his knuckles, then points his index and middle fingers to his eyes and outward toward me to warn that he's watching. "The day of the construction fire, Jillian's last run, I knew I'd never have to keep the threat. I'd never seen someone so tormented with worry. He tried to run into the building himself, and it took three of my men to hold him back. If you look at him, he's not a big guy, so you know how determined he was."

While others are chuckling, Jillian looks over at me with tears in her eyes. "You never told me you tried to come in there." She places her hand behind my neck and pulls me in for a kiss. "I love you."

EPILOGUE

After the first of the year, I found out why Anya never became a problem again. An article in the paper spoke of a new local businessman who was closing his stores before they opened due to his mistress coming forward with their love child. His wife divorced him, and they had no prenup because he was broke when they met, according to the article. Garth Howard was the businessman, and the distorted picture of the pregnant woman was most definitely Anya.

She didn't need me anymore; she had everything she wanted. I still feel sorry for the poor child she's going to raise.

Harrison and Carrie have a baby boy on the way, due

just after the new year. His name will be—of course—Kylo. When the lease ran out on their apartment, they bought a house not far from Jillian's. Well, I guess it's technically ours now. The girls reignited their friendship after the accident. When Carrie's test turned positive, Jillian was the first to know this time instead of the last like with the wedding.

We finally went on a double date with Adam and EJ, and it went so well it's become a monthly tradition. After Jyn was born, Jillian called Adam every day with some new worry. He was so patient with her when he had every right to tell her to leave him alone.

Stephan is Jyn's godfather. He helps us with her when we need time alone. And for our wedding gift, he sent us on a trip to Hawaii and kept Jyn while we were away. Jillian loves working for him and will continue to work full-time but has signed up with her old station to be a volunteer firefighter when needed.

Jillian received a settlement from the construction company. They'd used cheap wiring and materials that caused both the fire and the collapse. The construction company paid out to the business owners, Jillian, and Tucker's family in the end. A penny saved sent them to the poor house.

Her money—she calls it ours, but she was the one in the accident—went into a fund for Jyn's college tuition, and that of any siblings she may have. We had the talk and both agreed that we want to keep trying until we have at least one son.

Now as I sit here, I look at my beautiful wife asleep

on the couch, her soft snores the only sound in the room. Holding my chubby-cheeked little girl in my arms, I can't imagine a more perfect life than I have now.

There never was any doubt in my mind about Jillian.

As inebriated as I was that night on the sidewalk, the moment I saw Jillian Hartford, I knew I was going to marry her.

ACKNOWLEDGMENTS

To Hot Tree Publishing first and foremost for loving my submission enough to want to take it from a novella to full novel. Kristin, Olivia, Barbara, Paula, Sue, and Virginia, thank you for your kind words and help to make this novel the best it can be. Thank you, Becky, for believing in me and in my writing.

To my husband, who helped me to make sure all my *Star Wars* references were noted correctly. Not only does he check my references, but he lets me bounce scene ideas off him and helps me make sure they have the best punch possible. He's inspired many of the male characters in my book, and for this one, the love of *Star Wars* and the sarcastic wit of Sam is based on him. Thank you for being my muse and one of my biggest supporters, always.

To my parents, my mom, who still remains the one family member who has read all of my books. She promotes my books out to her friends and to strangers as well. My dad, who may not have read my books, but he still supports me by joining my mom at signings and bragging about me to whoever will listen.

And last but not least, to the loyal readers who have become friends, thank you for standing by me and keeping me confident in my writing. Your support is what means the most. Knowing there is someone out there enjoying my books keeps my love of writing alive.

ABOUT THE **AUTHOR**

Amy McClung was born in Nashville, TN. She is the second oldest of four girls and occasionally suffers from middle-child syndrome. She met the love of her life online in August of 2004, on his birthday of all days, and married him in September 2005.

Currently they have no human children, only the room full of colorful robots that transform into vehicles and the large headed Pop Funkos who represent their favorite characters. Collecting movies, shot glasses, Pop Funkos, and dust bunnies are some of her favorite pastimes.

Amy began writing in September of 2011 and independently published her first YA novel, "Cascades of Moonlight", book one of the Parker Harris series the following May. Her first book was a means of therapy for her, enabling her to escape reality for a while during a difficult transition in her life. To date she has published eleven novels, six of them with Hot Tree Publishing as well as being a part of two anthologies.

Amy loves to connect with her readers. You can reach her:

FACEBOOK: WWW.FACEBOOK.COM/AmyKMcclung
TWITTER: HTTPS://TWITTER.COM/AmythaMcclung
WEBSITE: AMYKMCCLUNG.BLOGSPOT.COM
INSTAGRAM: @AMYKMCCLUNG

ABOUT THE
PUBLISHER

Hot Tree Publishing opened its doors in 2015 with an aspiration to bring quality fiction to the world of readers. With the initial focus on romance and a wide spread of romance sub-genres, we envision opening up to alternative genres in the future.

Firmly seated in the industry as a leading editing provider to independent authors and small publishing houses, Hot Tree Publishing is the sister company to Hot Tree Editing, founded in 2012. Having established in-house editing and promotions, plus having a well-respected market presence, Hot Tree Publishing endeavors to be a leader in bringing quality stories to the world of readers.

Interested in discovering more amazing reads brought to you by Hot Tree Publishing? Head over to the website for more:

WWW.HOTTREEPUBLISHING.COM

9 781925 655568